Copyright © 2025 by Thea Atkinson

Print ISBN: 978-1-0699073-0-1

All rights reserved.

No part of this publication may be reproduced, distributed or transmitted in any form or by any means, including photocopying, recording, or other electronic or mechanical methods, without the prior written permission of the publisher, except as permitted by U.S. copyright law. For permission requests, contact thea at theaatkinson dot com

The story, all names, characters, and incidents portrayed in this production are fictitious. No identification with actual persons (living or deceased), places, buildings, and products is intended or should be inferred.

Permission not granted to use this content in AI training or works.

Cover Design by Christian Bentulan

First edition 2025

Special thanks to my beta readers.

Have you got your free ebook yet? Be sure to visit http://theaatkinson.com

Dedications

For every soul who has ever flown without wings, who has slipped into a story and found a world more honest, more vivid, more home than this one.

Chapter 1

I'VE NEVER REFUSED TO kill a man. Not for mercy. Not for guilt or love. Mortal, fae, shifter, troll. Whatever creed or creature I'm hired to kill, I do it without overthinking because emotion was never good for business.

There have been demi-gods, vampires and more over my long career. An angel once, though that was for pleasure, not payment. I will never regret that kill. It brought me joy instead of barter.

But killing isn't all I do. Sometimes it's simple larceny or surveillance, sometimes magic collection, the same as soldiers from the human mafia do for their bosses. Like them, I don't quibble over the jobs I take.

It's just that murder pays the best. And what they pay Ruby Morvannon for in the end. A good, clean kill with no loose ends.

So three days and six hours into tailing the high fae male whose commission had pulled me from the shadows of the Nocturnes and into the rot of the Iron Kingdom—I found myself crouched in a thicket beside a stone and stucco stable, shivering beneath the hush of twilight and wondering why I hadn't killed the bastard already.

The grass was slick with dew after a humid afternoon, and it tickled my forearm in ways that felt uncomfortably like fingers whispering over my skin. I had to shift my weight to avoid the long fronds.

I knew without counting that exactly five long fronds of weeds had laid beads of water on my bare arm. An odd, asymmetrical number that itched things in my psyche. I knew how far up my shins my leather breeks had gotten soaked from trampling through puddles and wet fields as I tried to keep out of sight during the trek. The clamminess of the material as it stuck to me in places nearly drove me mad.

I knew the distance between the stable where my mark sat and the place where I hid. I could notch back an arrow and hit him in the throat neatly with a single strike.

But I didn't.

Too much was riding on this hit. Stone was the son of the Shadow Court's leader, a court still in its infancy, and Aiofe, Queen of the Stygian Darkness herself, had called me forth to complete the job.

The seal of the vow between us swam in my blood with even greater intensity than it had when I'd first tracked him at his father's manse. It pulsed hard enough that I had to grit my teeth against the pressure as I sat in the thickets of brush around the stable.

The chill of the dew made my joints ache, the itching burn of the vow made me antsy. Envy wrinkled my brow at the way he conjured a fire to warm his hands while I hunkered deeper into my hiding place, tired and frustrated.

It had been an exhausting ordeal tailing him, mostly because he accompanied three mortal women. Since I'd not been commissioned to kill them, I wasn't about to do so for free unless it benefited me in some way.

That foolish decision cost me dearly. In three and a half days, they'd never left him alone, and he rarely slept. And because he didn't, I couldn't. I was now feeling the effects of exhaustion and cursing my choice to wait for him to be alone.

His family owned the Velvet Boar Tavern nestled into the hillside beside the stable. I knew that from my research.

Stone shifted from one foot to the other, putting me in mind of the moment I'd first seen him at the manse. There had been females there too, who scattered feed to the chickens and gathered herbs and vegetables wearing their homespun flax shifts or sometimes nothing at all. Some carried wood for the fireplaces. All were human.

The Shadow Court's possession of the Velvet Boar kept them as indentured prostitutes and servants until they wore out, which wasn't long. Humans had a limited shelf-life. Even in the depths of the Stygian Darkness, rumors spilled into eager ears.

Many of those indentured didn't even last a week.

I watched the firelight catch on the sharp angles of Stone's jaw. Hard and brutal, like the rest of his ilk. Like the rest of most fae from the Iron Kingdom, possessed of violent tendencies that took advantage of human frailty for their own pleasure.

And if those upper-realm fae of the Iron Court were violent, so much more so were those in its Shadow Court. Similar to the Nocturnes, I supposed. Not a friendly place for mortal creatures.

Movement from inside cast flickering shadows, reminding me of the women he'd ferried to this stable.

These three women were from that stable of indentured humans, and I found it curious that Stone brought them all the way from the manse, but did not deliver them to the barkeeper inside the tavern. He could have sauntered into the front door and deposited those women to the innkeeper's care and found a room above the tavern and been done with it all.

Except he didn't. He settled the women into beds of hay in the loft above the stabled horses before taking sentry below just inside the door. The horses shifted restlessly inside, hooves scuffing against the floorboards.

Occasionally, he let his gaze drift to the Velvet Boar as though he expected someone to relieve him of his burden, but then just as casually turned his eyes to the small fire he'd conjured in a circle of rocks beside the entryway.

I could have killed him then, notched an arrow from my quiver into my side-bow or slid through the shadows to slit his throat with my blade. I didn't. I stayed right where I was in that cushion of itchy grass and cold dew.

And that worried me. Hesitation was more dangerous in my vocation than an ill-placed strike. Hesitation meant death.

Being above ground for the first time in decades was an overwhelm of sounds and sights and touch and taste that had begun to boil over, itching through my skin and prickling my scalp. I had far too much stimulus, and I knew it.

The last time I'd seen the stars and moonlit sky, my sister was dying beneath the canopy of it. On a night fragrant with moon flowers and newly unfurled spring leaves, the tang of her blood and wasted magic coated my palate so thickly that I tasted it even now as I peered through the fronds of grass to the stable where Stone was carrying a bale of hay. He dropped it next to the maw of open door and settled onto it with feet outstretched.

Six feet of muscle in boiled leather. Blunt-fingered, square hands hardened by what I told myself was hours of swordplay.

I ran my fingers along the blade on my thigh, just as he arched backward, stretching his arms out as if presenting himself to me like a fowl for carving. The motion exposed the vulnerable line of his throat, and my muscles tightened reflexively, the same way they always did when a target revealed a weakness.

But something in my chest hitched, and for a moment, I gloried in the raw sense of power that movement revealed.

His broad shoulders were muscled and broad. When he straightened, his entire body went rigid. The gargantuan horse snorted. He paused for a long moment before he ran his hand over his hair, black in the deepest shades, cropped short in a bristling brush that most high fae would mock. Lazy decadence allowed them to keep their hair long and natural, even lashed into ribbons pretty enough to rival the females they wooed.

Not Stone. His close-cropped style marked him as a male of action and violence, a warrior who couldn't risk worrying about lush curls falling into his eyes during a heated battle. No prissy plaits for this massive creature, either.

I admired little, but I admired that about him. He wasn't a follower. As an underworld shifter who made her living killing and stealing, I could appreciate another who walked their own walk even when the path took them to the shoal of roads best left deserted.

He'd smiled five times in three days. Four polite. One sharp enough to show the points of his teeth. That one had looked more like a grimace as he'd paid a toll to a farmer for a bit of hard cheese he'd broken into three pieces and given to the women.

Cataloging each expression, whether it was a good-natured smile or a grin of fatigue, mattered. The appearance of either meant he would be distracted enough for me to strike with the least risk. I needed to know what each of them looked like.

All those things told me a lot about the mark I tailed. At least that's what I told myself as I watched him.

Despite myself, I wondered what the calloused pads of his fingers would feel like if they should brush against my hand in battle. Would I cringe? Flinch? Feel a blessed bit of nothing?

That would be the best, I decided. My skin always felt weird and electric when someone touched me. As though it could sense the vibrations of their thoughts when they first met me.

And I did not want to know what anyone thought of me. I'd heard enough in my lifetime to know exactly what those would sound like.

So, I eyeballed him as he pulled a grey-ware pot from his pack and hung it from a triangle of fire irons in the center of the slow-burning fire carved into a pit of dirt at the stable's entrance. He tossed a few chunks of dried meat in with the shriveled root vegetables from his pack.

I caught a whiff of the meat on the stolid air and thanked the gods my stomach didn't growl in response.

Reaching for the bow beside me, I watched without blinking. If he didn't move, I could easily take him out, steal his stew and be gone before the women knew he was dead.

The feel of the yew wood, smooth in my grip after all these centuries, was a comfort. I rolled onto my side. Slow movements. Painstakingly, achingly deliberate. Brushing aside the foliage to notch the arrow point into enough space that I could aim slightly upward, keeping the bow out of range of the earth so it didn't vibrate as I released and queer the release.

I had a perfect view. I'd been quiet enough that he hadn't even looked into the darkness to where I lay.

From this angle, I had the cleanest shot—straight through the throat, severing the artery and windpipe in one breath. No warning. No chance for him to call fire or steel. A perfect kill.

My fingers should have tingled with anticipation. Instead they trembled, a microscopic shift only I would notice. A hitch of some sort rippled through me. Exhaustion, I told myself, though the rationalization scraped at my psyche.

I blew out a long breath, calming my nerves, then inhaled a second draft of air twice the length. Closed my eyes. Opened them again.

Then I caged that breath as I pulled back, letting the oxygen dance with the adrenaline. When I eased the air out again, it was with a soft sigh as I prepared to let the arrow fly.

The shot was perfectly aligned. My fingers thrummed, ready, against the bowstring.

Stone's head lifted, just slightly — as if he sensed the tension in the air.

And even before I'd let go, I knew I'd made a horrible mistake.

Chapter 2

KILLING HAD A WAY of deadening things that had nothing to do with violence. A creature's last breath is a humbling moment. A powerful instant where everything funnels down to a speck of energy, one that contains everything in the essence of the creature itself. Potential. Past. A thousand paths from each small decision converged and tightened into a cluster of blackness so complete, no light pointed the way out.

The sort of darkness that the Stygian Darkness was made of, the sort that the queen of all that pitch black drank like fine wine.

I knew that sensation, that taste of cherries and cloves and power, because it hit me hard the moment Aiofe called me forth into her throne room deep in the heart of Kumara.

As the shadows fell away from me, she wasted no time declaring her reason for pulling me from the transient leyline of the Nocturnes where I hid in silence.

"I have a kill for you," she'd said the moment the shadows left me and allowed me to take shape enough to bow to her in the chilling gloom.

Behind her, a long, gloomy corridor led to a set of worn granite steps. Black-steel cells lined the walls, and in places loomed out from the darkness. Aiofe herself stood framed between the corridor's mouth and the writhing stretch of dungeon where snakes of arms and hands clamored for contact.

I knew better than to acknowledge them. I pretended my eyesight--honed from generations inside the darkness of the Nocturnes—was too weak to make out the faces carved into the walls of each cell or the bones embedded into the mortar.

A Sidhe had to keep her secrets, even from the queen of the darkness that bore her.

What I did was bow my head and keep my eyes downcast. A purple beetle scuttled between my boots to disappear into the blacksteel dungeon.

"Rise," Aiofe said, her voice tinged with impatience. "I have no stomach for the banal courtesies of fae courts."

I dared look up then, surprised to see her clothed in a fae appearance instead of her true hellhound form. From the thigh-high red boots to the lacy black chemise that barely concealed an inch square of the lovely form she presented, she seemed wholly fae. Deceptively beautiful. What she was beneath that shape was far more dangerous than any fae I'd known.

Her hands were planted on her hips, pulling apart the grand leather cinched waist jacket, the cloak over that, and her eyes narrowed as they took me in. The lethal gaze wormed with crimson, like a trail of blood coiling around her irises. It took everything in me not to react to the sight or to the intensity of her gaze.

So long as she didn't touch me, I wouldn't flinch.

"Ruby of the Nocturnes," she said in a voice thick with smoky husk, as though brimstone lined her throat. "You commit violence for barter?"

My jaw clenched as I considered the words and the spirit of them, trying desperately to work out what she wanted to hear. Discerning emotion and motive behind expressions and timbre of voice was the hardest part of my vocation. In all my centuries, I'd not mastered either. But I squared my shoulders and thrust my chin upward just the same, the easiest response I could find that might be acceptable.

"I have bartered lives for coin, yes," I said carefully. "And I have accepted gold for lesser tasks. What service is it that you require of me, my queen?"

Formal, so very formal, but the one thing I had learned was that protocol was a friend in the face of uncertainty.

She waved away the title with an irritated gesture, that crimson serpent in her eyes flashing as though the fire in her veins had found an escape route. "I have need of an assassin."

The way she waited, then, holding my gaze, I could make out the hellhound form bleeding through the facade of luminescent fae. Sussing me out, trying to see if I might be shocked that she'd need someone to do her work for her.

"He's from the upper realms," she said, her throat tight with some emotion I couldn't name. I decided it was interest, because her chin tilted upward the same way my sister's always did when she tried to bait me into an argument.

If Queen Aiofe was baiting me, a lowly mercenary from the Nocturnes of her Own Darkness, to see how I would react to a chance of rising from the shadow realm, she didn't give me time to provide it. She swirled the long crimson leather cloak around her torso, covering her body below the neck.

No doubt she yearned to let go of the fae form she held. I understood the compulsion. Shifting took energy best conserved for other things, and holding a secondary form took a lot of power, even for the queen of the darkness.

"I have a steep price for murder," I said.

Her mouth twitched, though I didn't know what the movement meant. Disgust? Approval? Was she angry that I wouldn't offer a deal to the regent of the realm?

The cloak tightened around her neck, and a long claw snuck out around the edge, buckling the fabric.

"You realize I have the power to grant something no one else can. Something more precious than mere gold."

My heart stuttered. There was only one thing that precious in my mind, and it terrified me that she might know it. That *thing* was something I wouldn't let myself consider, let alone confess aloud.

Fae didn't die the way mortals did. Their life force was tied to the magic in their blood and marrow. They wasted, and in that wasting, the form of the fae went to the Darkness. To Aiofe. Never truly dead but not alive either. Just...existing the way a bit of steam did just before it evaporated.

My lungs refused to expand as I tried once more to read her expression and failed. I ended up just standing there awkwardly, running my palm over the blade handle sheathed on my hip. Only when she pivoted on her heel, relieving me of the need to search her face, could I breathe again.

I chose my words carefully then, because my chest had grown so unexpectedly tight that I could barely breathe.

"I imagine there are many gifts you could offer."

There was a pause in her step at my comment. She glanced at me over her shoulder. The waft of cinnamon and strong cloves, of fire and smoke coiled about me like tentacles as the darkness seethed around her—movements of her thralls clamoring for her attention from the shadows.

I swallowed through a tight throat. She was trying to cower me with that look. But it was a pulse of her power, and no more. Her way of reminding me that in the cloud of shadow, in that throng of deadened, wasted fae who languished at her beck and call, a shape I knew and loved was in her possession.

It took effort push away the thought of that shape, and why it was there. It took sheer will to swallow down the gutted, chewy balsam sap feeling in the pit of my stomach back down into the well I'd created explicitly for emotions I refused to feel.

Struggling to hold my composure, I held my breath as a large chair wafted in from the shadows to take its place behind her as gently as a breeze before conjuring itself into a bone-backed throne with ivory legs gnarled into feet thick enough to support several hellhounds.

My fingers automatically skimmed my forearm, testing for the shape of bone and ivory beneath my wrist. A memory tried to rise from the depths. A boy's screams tried to fill my ears.

Both of them, I squashed mercilessly. If she was trying to cower me, it wouldn't be with things long done. There was already enough anxiety to make my legs quake.

She circled around me, the hem of her crimson cloak brushing the stone in a whisper of fabric so soft it sounded like hushed threats as she paused behind me. A sting rose between my shoulder blades, like the branding of hot iron along my spine. I caged a gasp between my teeth and with a chuckle; she strolled past me to settle onto the seat of her throne. Her baleful glance at me made my knees buckle as she crossed her legs. The fae shape of her limbs instead of hound's legs held a graceful curve in those long boots made of rippling leather.

"You wonder how I found you when the Nocturnes is so well shadowed," she said as she watched my face. "You must know that no matter how efficiently your Madre cloisters it, I know well every inch of this darkness."

I held my neutral mask because I wasn't sure which expression she would most expect to see. I certainly wasn't going to speak about the things the Madre did to remain beneath the queen's radar.

She rolled her eyes, obviously disappointed with the lack of affect in my face. "Of course, you won't ask. You want to know what I know about you, and yet you don't banter. You're not a talkative sort, are you Ruby Morvannon?"

I wanted badly to shift my feet, but I remained still.

"I've never found a time when chatter kept me alive."

Aiofe smiled with her teeth showing. "Indeed," she said. "But perhaps this one time, you will."

The shadows around her shuddered, suggesting forms and shapes trying to emerge from the darkness to be seen. They whispered all around me from within those blacksteel cells and the shadows behind the throne as they cast off the scent of ozone from whatever magic they'd managed to recharge over their time in the Darkness, offering it to the queen who forced them to move as though they were attached to marionette strings.

Those wasted spirits had spent centuries regaining their lost power. Relinquishing any of that magic was a sacrifice. All so she could intimidate me into offering her a bit of chatter.

It didn't add up, and so I said the first thing that came to my mind, unnerved as I was, knowing my sister was likely one of those in the shadows, giving up magic that had cost her years to gather.

"It's no secret why you chose me," I said.

Aiofe's eyebrow lifted, intrigued, it seemed, at my choice of small talk. Nonplussed, I continued.

"Anonymity," I said. "The Nocturnes is small. No one would know or recognize the Ruby Morvannon it birthed. And that means the fae you have marked is well-connected."

I thought of the lifetime I'd spent in the Nocturnes, a small place cloaked by the Madre's magic, aiming desperately to gain enough power to rise from the depths of the darkness to some sort of light. It was a source, our source, the place I needed to touch down in so I could recharge my magic. A place where I never felt safe after Enyali died.

My sister's face came to me then, the only kindness I'd known, and yet I'd barely hugged her in the years I'd known her. Something I regretted now. A regret Aiofe sensed and used as she watched me with an intensity that made my feet shift, just a hair apart. Defensive as she considered her response.

The queen's smile was wolfish. "Your mark is the son of the Shadow Court's master. A power in his own right. Terran is grooming him to be his second, so he possesses loyalties that go beyond what you and I might enjoy. He goes by the name Stone," she said, ignoring my comment. "You'll think it apt once you see him. You might even think he carved his body to match the moniker."

She stretched her leg out, admiring it before crossing it over her knee. That she'd taken her eyes off me told me exactly how badly she wanted him dead.

She didn't need to say she wanted this Stone's magic. The hunger for it was plain in her eyes the moment she named him. Holding as many thralls as she did in stasis took a lot of power, and yet she had enough to hold the entirety of the Stygian Darkness together.

Obviously, there was something more she wanted from that magic, and whatever it was, the problem could be solved with his death. Exactly what that problem was, was not my concern. But the fae she held in her dungeons was.

So I bargained with her. Stone's life for my sister's.

And as I did, something in me twisted—deep, stupid, unwanted—as though this job would be more than a job. It would be my ruin.

Chapter 3

HAPPENSTANCE CAN BE AS evil as the darkest of fae sorcerers, and the moment my fingers sought to release the arrow toward Stone's throat, a woman stepped out of the darkness of the stable and into the light behind him.

Long-haired. Flashing blue eyes that contrasted with the jet of her locks even in the magic fire that cast its light toward her.

She was fast, faster than I expected for a human woman. And silent, apparently, because Stone didn't so much as flinch as she crept behind him and lifted a broad blade with both hands, aiming for the back of his neck.

It was a ridiculous angle, and couldn't possibly result in more than a painful stab into the muscle of his shoulder. And yet, it was the moment that changed everything.

I didn't hesitate.

One small adjustment to my aim, perhaps a hair's width and no more, and I let the arrow escape with all the noise of a gasp.

It struck the blade in the woman's hand, forcing her to drop the weapon to the ground with a noiseless sound. She fumbled backward almost elegantly as she realized what had happened and quickly reassessed. Her scream cut off as her hands flew to her mouth, shoving fingers inside to cut off any noise. With a spin as graceful as her backward pirouette, she fled to the stable, where the other two women had already appeared, drawn no doubt by the noise. They gathered her into comforting embraces and disappeared together behind a boarded-up stall.

A soft curse escaped my lips as I ducked down into the gorse and shrubs. Dragging in quick breaths as though starved of all air, I rolled onto my back and clutched the bow to my chest. Squeezing my eyes closed, I berated myself for the hasty decision to save the fae from the mortal's attack. He would know I was out here now. I'd never get another chance.

I tried to tell myself that I'd done it because I wasn't paid to take out a mortal, but I knew our strikes would have been simultaneous and redoubled my chance of success.

And yet...I had shifted my aim a hair to the left.

I was still shivering with adrenaline when I heard his gruff voice calling out to me from his place at the stable, beyond the thicket where I lay.

"You missed," he said, his voice like gravel and bits of heated coal. A good voice, I thought. One that made me feel warm in the cradle of my hiding place.

The swallow that lodged on a hard lump in my throat pushed a puddle of water back into my cheeks. I had to shift into shadow, pull everything I was into a puddle of darkness and straddle the ley lines of realms, and I had to do it now before he stomped into the bushes to find me.

The woman inside was weeping loudly. Her companions were just as loud as they tried to prise information out of her. If I was quick, I could use their chaos as cover while I gathered my magics enough to cloak me from sight.

Too late, I heard the rustling of grass and shrubbery nearby, the heavy breath of someone who hadn't labored over movement but had suffered a jolt of adrenaline. Heavy but deliberate steps, like the feet were accustomed to stealth.

I opened my eyes to see him standing over me.

This close, he was even larger than I thought. He'd stand at least half a foot over me if I got to my feet.

Those eyes I'd thought aquamarine during the day from a few hundred feet away were more royal in the darkness, but maybe that was because the pupils were so large. Like an owl taking in a mouse. The smell of caramel swept over me, buttery warm molasses and sugar. For a second I couldn't breathe. Lightning bugs flashed in my chest.

"You think I haven't noticed you trailing us the last few days," he said. Not a question. He obviously didn't expect me to answer.

I pushed myself to an upright position, planting the bow next to me in the grass. It would be useless this close. What I needed was my knife. From behind us, the woman was still wailing loud enough that I could almost taste her tears.

"I didn't miss," I said, lifting my chin.

A flash, only that, but the smile had come out to play. Not the tight full-toothed one that showed annoyance. The half smile. The one he reserved for the woman who had just tried to kill him. I tasted bitter salt at the thought of her. Ridiculous that he should save his perfect smile for a mortal.

His gaze flicked sideways to where my hand was burrowing into the grass.

"I wouldn't bother searching for the knife," he said. "It's not there."

My fingers froze. The blade. But how?

This time, his smile broke out in full. Mockery, then. That's what that smile meant, because somehow, impossibly, I'd shot my blade from the woman's hand, and he knew it.

Abandoning pretense and doing my best to disguise my unease, I stood. "Considering I just saved your life, you don't seem very grateful."

A hint of a smile. "Grateful?" He said. "Exactly what did you save me from?"

My mouth twisted as I brushed the grass from my leathers. Looking up, I realized he had at least six inches on me. I pointed toward the barn. "She was going to kill you."

He laughed, a dark, melodic sound that reminded me of the thralls in Aiofe's dungeons.

"She wouldn't have killed me," he said.

"How do you know that?"

His shrug moved his shoulders so slightly I wasn't sure I'd actually seen it. "Because I asked her to do that."

"To trick me into showing myself," I said, realizing I'd no doubt given myself away days earlier. "A pretty big risk for a fae, considering what you do with those women."

Another shrug. "The only question of risk was whether you would shoot her or me." He crossed his arms lazily, suggesting he wasn't the least bit worried that I'd attack him. "Truth be told, she wouldn't have minded had it been her. She's broken now, you see. A woman of art from her realm. A dancer of sorts. Those sorts don't have such violence in them, and in her case, it would tear a hole in whatever soul she has left."

He was unhinged. It was just that simple. No one in their right mind would risk their own death that way unless they were over confident or plain mad. My eyes shuttered as I considered this new development, not sure whether to be impressed or afraid.

When he held out his hand, my blade sat on his palm, bone-carved handle pointing toward me.

I looked it over, not daring to pluck it from his hand. At least not right then. I wasn't foolish enough to take that chance.

I ran several scenarios through my head, dropping it by the fire as I'd crept about the camp, laying it down as I drank from a river and forgetting to pick it back up.

"How did you get that from me without me knowing?"

His eyebrows inched up. "Maybe I'm just very fast."

"Fast enough to slide it out from my pack and give it to your mortal woman so she could pretend to kill you," I said, echoing the truth out loud finally. I tried not to think that he'd also have had to be near invisible and scentless to get that blade from me without me knowing. There were better questions to ask.

"To what end?"

"To see what you'd do."

His palm was still outstretched, and he waggled the blade at me. I snatched it from his hand and brushed his fingers, feeling as if he would curve his hand to trap mine and almost letting it linger. But then my hand came away, and I shoved the blade into its sheath, where it belonged. No sense even considering the assassination at this point with the loss of surprise.

"Why?" he asked, his gaze lingering on the pulse in my throat and making it ratchet up.

"Why, what?"

"Why didn't you shoot me? You're obviously trailing me for a reason." He indicated the stash of weapons lying on the ground at our feet. "You've brought more than enough arms to take me down from a distance as well as close up. Why didn't you take the hit?"

I thought of Enyali then, recalling the moment in Kumara when I knew I could free her with that one shot, and my shoulders sagged. It should have been easy. A half-second of hesitation had changed everything.

Why indeed? It wasn't like me to waste an arrow. The thought of pulling one out of an extra, unexpected body did something to my insides that made them shake.

But that wasn't why I'd altered the course of the aim by an inch.

"I could have done it at your father's manse," is what I said, because I couldn't find an answer to his question that would satisfy me.

He nodded slowly, as though digesting this information for the first time. "Ah, but too many soldiers there," he said. "Not to mention my brothers. Both of them would tear you limb from limb and take their time digesting you." His head inclined down, just a bit, so that he looked at me from beneath shuttered lashes, his voice as dry as winter corn husks. "And then there is my father."

I had to swallow down the strange unease in my belly, like fireflies flashing heat into the darkness.

My chin thrust up, defiant.

"I blended in," I insisted. I had. Hard as it was to disappear into the servant folk of the manse, with those lesser fae mistaking me for one of the pleasure females who hung about properties like that looking for a few coins for a moment's work, I'd managed to stay near invisible amongst the elite.

Quite a feat, considering hiding in plain sight was not my forte. I usually got in, got things done, and got out All under the cover of shadow and stealth.

"You think my father's servants and grunts don't know every face, every creed of fae and human that belong to the place?" He snuffed in disdain, and even then the noise made the small of my back tingle.

I blinked at him, doing everything I could to keep from arguing. I was caught, and I knew it, but that didn't mean I had to make myself look pathetic. If only I could keep my mouth shut.

He tilted his head to the side, eyeballing me with that penetrating gaze. "You're not a very good assassin. I should have let the mortal woman slit your throat while you slept."

That rankled. "I haven't slept," I said hotly.

He laughed outright then, a sound that felt strangely intimate, like the mockery of one lover to another. "Oh, you slept. Irina said she had to swat a fly away that kept landing on your tongue."

A nerve beneath my eye twitched. There had been a moment in the deep woods when I'd found a hollow in a tree to hide in while they made camp beside a river. It had been warm, if not damp. And I'd been so damned tired. An image of me snapping my mouth shut as I snorked myself wide awake reminded me I'd felt like something was off, that I'd felt an energy near me that didn't belong. I'd bitten down hard enough on my tongue to taste blood.

The panic that shot up from my belly to my throat at the thought that someone had touched my weapons, that someone had gotten close to me without my knowing, sent flames of heat to my skull and burned there behind my eyes.

My spine went rigid. "Irina is lucky I aimed for the blade handle and not her eye."

With a soft hum in his throat, he toed the bow toward my feet. It rolled over, striking me in the shin.

"If you believe you could have done that before I intervened, then you haven't done your research."

I realized he wanted me to pick up my weapon. Fine. I needed something to do with my hands anyway because they kept trying to wring themselves out between us.

Without taking my eyes from his, I stooped and reclaimed it along with the quiver and settled them into place on my back. If he was going to let me go, best I make him think I'd learned my lesson like a terrible, ineffective would-be assassin. Then await another opportunity.

"I didn't have time to research," I complained in an affected plaintive voice, using his mistaken belief in my capabilities against him as casually as my lungs expanded for breath.

"No time?" he asked, shifting on his feet.

The look he gave me then suggested I'd managed to garner his interest if not sympathy. Either would do just fine. For all the good it would do him.

Outwardly, I knew my face remained stoic, but inside I was smiling. To keep it that way, I dropped my gaze to my feet. That should look like shame, shouldn't it?

"I'm a hunter of sorts," I said truthfully. "Wild boar cocks fetch a king's ransom from the potion makers in the marketplaces."

That was true as well. Let him argue the fact if he wanted, and for a moment, the way he canted his head to the side, I thought he would. He certainly seemed to be thinking the statement over, because his gaze moved to my throat almost leisurely, locking on my hammering pulse.

My fingers curled into my palms as he watched me, and a slow smile threaded its way across his face. One that rankled, because I couldn't for the life of me figure out what could be so humorous.

"I don't know which of the potion makers has put out a warrant for *my* cock, but I assure you, while it has provided magical experiences for many a female, I have but one, and its limited supply makes it insufficient to power any potion to the degree that trying to take it from me would be a worthwhile investment."

His eyes flicked to my face. "Now the goods within the sack," he tilted his head as he seesawed his hand between us. "They are copious and unlimited. In which case, I'm happy to oblige."

A hum of threat in his voice under-painted something far huskier. Something that made my breath hitch even as he inched closer, so subtly that I wasn't prepared for the panic that flared up in my chest. For one moment there was a burst of excitement that rang in my ears, and then—a lightning strike, sending up a warning shot to the darkness.

That swift, subtle movement lit all sorts of unwanted images behind my eyelids. The feel of a different blade gripped in a fist as it wavered over a youth's skin. The faintest yielding of flesh as it echoed down the length of metal and bone. Revulsion coated my palate to war with the heat his words brought to my cheeks.

The taste of duty and loathing dredged the swamp of my memories, trying to pull out the taste of blood and smoke, and I sucked in a breath of air as though starving for it. I found a thin strand of willpower dangling up into the light and grabbed for it, frantic to have something to cling to, knowing if I didn't hang on I'd either strike out or drop to my knees in a blathering mess.

That was when Stone's face swam in front of me, bringing me back from the brink, reminding me where I was, and I fought back. The way a bound captive would. With vitriol and language, my only safety line, a sanctuary built on sandy earth.

"Oh, have no fear," I ground out as the world shifted and rebalanced beneath my feet. "I wouldn't touch your cock long enough to slice it from your crotch even if I was promised enough ransom to install me in a mansion."

His mouth twitched, but he didn't back away, and I'd be damned if I would either. I hadn't cowered before Aiofe days earlier or in my duty a generation ago. I wouldn't now. The earth beneath my feet held firm. My knees built scaffolding beneath me. I faced the intensity of his gaze with a controlled, deadpan mask even though my whole body felt like it was trembling.

And yet, despite my determination, when he extended his hand, I flinched before I could stop myself. A quirk of his mouth told me he saw it, but his fingers rounded my shoulder to brush the quiver instead of my arm, and everything in me sagged in relief.

"You've been tracking me for days," he said, dropping his voice almost conspiratorially. "Is that weapon merely for defense or were you waiting for the right moment." He cast a long look toward the stable, where I sensed the women had gathered and were watching us.

His feet shuffled, spacing themselves apart defensively. "There is no charlatan in the markets paying you," he said as he pulled free one of my arrows. "There is no special elixir that my body, my organs, or my seed will empower. Is there?" This last was said with a note of command, except he didn't wait for an answer.

Using the arrow to point at the stable, he continued, "You could have killed Irina but didn't. You could have removed all of the mortal females as witnesses long before tonight and taken your shot of me. You have enough arrows." He nodded at the quiver.

I shrugged in my tunic, rolling my shoulders. "I wasn't paid to kill them."

Eyebrows rose an inch on his forehead. "So you confess to mercenry, then."

My jaw jutted to the side, clamping my teeth around the answer. I thought of my sister, not more than a shade of pale energy lost in Aiofe's dungeons, being fed upon for every bit of magic she managed to reclaim for herself. I overlaid it with the memory of her dancing in the shadow gardens of the Nocturne, picking blood-heart flowers and squeezing their nectar into her scrying bowls. Something inside me twisted.

I held my tongue until his sigh got lost in the sound of my arrow breaking in two as he snapped it against his leg. If breaking the iron wood shaft with a single hand hurt, he made no sign.

"I'll tell you what you won't say out loud," he said. "Some sloppy, ignorant rival to the Shadow Court decided to try to instigate war by hiring a soft-hearted, poorly trained hunter as an unlikely assassin to its leaders son."

He stepped back finally, giving me room to breathe, space to gather my energy. "And because it is of the fault of that unnamed rival, I'll give you the opportunity to call him out."

I would have laughed at the misrepresentation of my skill set, except it benefited me to let him think so poorly of me. At least for the time being.

Because unwittingly, he'd just given me the means to kill him.

Chapter 4

NAMING AIOFE THE QUEEN of the Stygian Darkness would be my own lingering death. Even above the realm, in the world of light and shifting shadow, where cold and warmth tangled to create wavering touches over flesh aching for sensation, no fae from any of the kingdoms would be so stupid as to incriminate the mistress of the dark in anything.

To admit to her being the procurer of an attempted assassination of the Shadow Court's would-be second would be to beg for a painful death at her hand.

She, who commanded the shadows where the lingering shells of our souls went when wasted of the magic within, a place where we were no longer full fae or sidhe but ghosts of the things we were without the fascial foundation of magic.

Rumor was she had possession of some true dead fae, who had succumbed to a violent, sudden end. That she refused to let them cross into the spirit of nature as was their right.

So, I hedged, because I knew the sort of power she owned, and I needed him to think I was exactly the novice he believed.

"I'd rather just be left to admit defeat and walk away if it's all the same to you."

I took a step sideways, intending to shoulder my way past him and into the depths of the shadows where I could pull my magic around me and be gone to his eyes. But he side-stepped at the same moment, seeming to sense my movement before I made it.

"I've committed no crime. No mortal women were harmed. You live yet."

"And yet our business is not finished," he said and extended his arm in the direction of the fire, still blazing a warm-looking blue. "Please," he said. "If you haven't slept, then perhaps you haven't eaten either."

There was no mockery in his tone, but I went rigid just the same.

My eyes betrayed me as they traced the line hungrily to where the pot steamed in the light of the stable. I was sure it hadn't done that earlier. As though he were manipulating the air and light just so to make my stomach growl. Crafty. I couldn't smother the sounds my stomach made.

And there, crowded around the fire, stood the three mortal women. One of them, Irina, glared at me even though I was sure she couldn't see me.

"The purveyor of your death has my sister," I said.

The very air shifted at the words, and it took all my willpower to keep my gaze on the woman crossing her arms beside the fire and not to the hulking mass of energy beside me.

"Extortion," he said.

I adjusted the quiver on my back as I let my attention settle on him once more. "You understand my dilemma, then."

He let out a soft rush of air in a sigh that was both resigned and frustrated. "I know the strategy well. My family puts it to great use."

Sketching a slight bow that somehow made him only look even taller, he continued, "Come share our meal and you can tell me what sort of fool would ransom your loved one with my life."

My throat fluttered with excitement. It couldn't be this easy, could it? Perhaps I had the wrong male. Perhaps one of the other large and brooding bastards I'd caught lurking around the mansion had been the correct Stone and this was one of the brothers. Flint perhaps, or the eldest, a brutal fae who went by the name of Blade.

My hesitation seemed to confuse the fae in front of me. He looped my elbow with his and guided me along with him through the grass. My lungs felt too full of air.

"We have plenty," he said. "The women...they don't like to consume anything unless they catch it or collect it themselves." I could feel him shaking his head. "Something about eating and drinking in fairyland binding them to our world."

He laughed good-naturedly then, and it was so startling that I peered up at him as we trudged through the grass and broke onto the hard pack of the paddock.

"I mean..." he said, gesturing toward the women dressed in threadbare tunics. "They are bound for sure, but it has nothing to do with the food." The chuckle died in his throat as he gave them an assessing glance.

I followed his line of sight to where the women had huddled together beside the fire. "Irina calls us spirits, but the others...they have a more cunning understanding of us. It will make it difficult to let them return to their world after all they've seen."

He sounded sad.

"So it's true?" I asked, surprised at the comment. "The humans know of us?"

We had stopped at the perimeter, and the smell of manure was stronger now, the faces of the women more clear.

I darted a look at Irina and dropped my voice so none of them could hear me. "I've heard rumors that they believe we steal their young and use the magic of the act to bring ourselves to their world, but that never made sense."

I leveled the women with a disparaging glance. "Can they be that primitive that they could know of us and not realize we have our own magic?"

I'd been in the mortal realm few times over my lifetime, and while the humans were primitive indeed, they no longer lived in pit houses and caves. Their dwellings of stone and thatch resembled the homes and taverns of the baser fae. So much so that I believed some fae had brought the knowledge to them like Prometheus offering fire.

"I've not been above realm for a long time," I said thoughtfully. "But the last time I was in the light, our worlds looked similar. Horses. Carriages. Homes of stone and thatch."

His arms tightened against his sides. The hand nearest me curled into a fist.

"But they are not the same. We have magic and they can never truly know it exists." There was a pause, as though he was thinking before he continued. "They can't truly know of us."

He struck out then, leaving me behind as though he didn't realize I could simply draw on him and be done.

Maybe he didn't care or was foolish enough to think I pitied the women the same as he seemed to.

For a moment, I considered it, but then Irina disengaged from the group and strolled toward him, meeting up with us long before we reached the fire.

The flames couldn't have been more searing than the sensation in my throat as he reached out for her and stroked her hair. I clenched my hand over the strap of the quiver and before I could process why I was doing it, I pitched myself toward them, brushing past brusquely and heading for the fire.

"What have you in the pot, then?" I asked, too bluntly it seemed, judging by the glare Irina shot me as I peered down into the stew of meat and vegetables.

"You're going to feed her?" the human demanded in a voice that should have earned her a backhand across the cheek.

But Stone merely tucked a finger beneath her chin and lifted her gaze to his. "She's hungry. Do you remember a time when you needed bread?"

She turned to watch him as he prowled close to the fire, stopping on the other side of me. Her posture was rigid. Whatever bread she'd needed in her life was long forgotten as she swept me with a hateful glare.

"After she nearly killed you?"

Incredulous, that tone. I may not understand much human emotion, but I understood that. She thought he should kill me, not show me comfort. And the way he laughed at her words made me rage inside, because it suggested he thought the notion just as crazy. But for different reasons.

"I wouldn't use the word nearly," he countered as he caught my eye across the fire.

She brushed at her skirts with an awkward hand as if she wanted to argue, and I realized she was favoring it as she stalked silently back to the other women and took her place in the middle. All three of them blinked at us like owls in the pale light. A shiver ran through me, not because it was a silent judgment, but because I knew very well how owls were used by the Darkness for their own ends.

Stone gestured at a bale of hay that sat just inside the stable door, bidding me take a seat.

"These Indentured have lost all trust," he said to me. "It's not their fault that they prefer I slit your throat and move on."

The way he said it so casually made me give him a second look. There was no remorse in his voice regarding my desired death, and I wasn't surprised that he had killed before. But there was something else in his voice, a faint underpinning of emotion that I couldn't name, a huskiness that seemed more about those women losing trust than in slitting a stranger's throat.

I adjusted the quiver, refusing to take it off as I sat on the corner, legs splayed wide but with my feet planted firmly in case I needed to rise quickly. After centuries in the dark, my vision allowed me to see things that the daylight fae, even with their magics, couldn't. And the women looked positively murderous.

Smoothing my palm along my thigh, I said, "And yet you haven't slit my throat."

"I haven't *yet*," he agreed. "I do things in my own time."

He bent to spoon a bit of stew into the bowl I'd seen him use earlier. Rising, he pinned that intense gaze on mine again and held it as his legs devoured the distance between us in three paces.

The waft of smoke and woods came along with him, and when he passed me the bowl, I had to stretch for it. The warmth of the pottery, combined with the unexpected soft touch of his fingers before they relinquished the vessel to me, made me draw back too fast. I almost spilled it, and only caught myself just before it upended in my lap.

I pretended the near accident was part of adjusting myself on the hay, pushing back more firmly so I had more lap to place the bowl on. His admission that he was postponing my inevitable execution didn't surprise me. I expected that. Counted on it, even.

But I was surprised that he was feeding me before he did it. He could torture the information he wanted out of me if he wanted. But he was offering me succor. It made no sense.

At least, not until I skimmed the women in the dark again, and noticed the way they kept looking over their shoulders at the tavern and then back again at Stone.

"These women trust you," I said, drawing his attention away from my awkward near mishap.

"They do."

I glanced past him to where they whispered together, Irina's gaze lingering too long on Stone's back. I'd seen possessiveness. Lust. Rage. All those emotions that took little emotional fortitude to recognize. It was the subtle things I had a hard time with.

But in her face, I saw something I'd not witnessed enough to recognize, even though it was as intense as those base, easily recognized emotions. This time, I saw love.

I lifted the bowl to my mouth and peered at him over the rim as I sniffed at the contents. Herbs aplenty, though I'd not seen him add any. The fragrances cloyed on my palate.

"They are fools," I said.

Rather than arguing, as I expected of him, he used his hip to shove me over on the hay bale and took up most of the room. I had to lift the bowl high in the air to avoid spilling it. The feel of his thigh against mine was disconcerting.

"Those women have endured years of fae indenture and have survived," he said so low I knew he was trying to avoid them hearing. "I have been tasked with delivering them to the tavern, where they will serve the whims of high fae and low fae alike, so long as they can pay the coin required to the Shadow Court's coffers."

I looked askance at him. "They are hardy stock," I guessed.

He nodded, a flare moving in the depths of his aquamarine eyes with a hint of copper ringing them. "They've proved they can withstand the rigors of fae life."

His insinuation was clear, and the horror of it echoed in his expression.

I snorted at the thought that he should worry over the indelicacy of spelling it out for me. "And so they are most likely to earn out a decent tenure under the brutality of fae males of every sort."

"They are the types who will bring in the most coin before they succumb," he said, adding emphasis to the last word.

"Like I said: fools." I sniffed at the air as I lifted my chin toward them. "I'd take my own life before allowing such atrocities just to die at the hands of a bastard anyway."

"Perhaps it's easy for a near immortal fae to make that statement."

He took the bowl from me and put it to his lips, watching me over the rim as he took a long gulp of the watery stew. "They are made differently. They cling to life because they have only the one while we waste and regenerate in the depths of the Stygian Darkness before we find life once more."

He let loose a long sigh. "Sometimes I think that's their magic."

I sucked the back of my teeth, making a noise that lifted his eyebrows.

"Have you ever met anyone who has claimed to return from the Darkness?" I asked him, and when he didn't respond, I pressed the point further. "Those fae who have found true death and been reborn as trees or bees. You think it's every fae's fate?"

I laughed coldly. "Not all nature is beautiful as the things you see in your light world, Dayling. Some nature is cruel. Blight. Plague. The destructive nature of hurricanes and eruptions. These energies are as much part of nature as light and peace. Some fae are meant to regenerate a thousand times as such evil things before they may be born again of the fae form."

"This is well known," he said, with a grudging note in his voice that only galled me more.

"Ah but you, Dayling. You think wasting is better than existing as a hurricane or disease." I took the bowl back and drained it, leaving the last morsels of meat in the bowl. "In the Darkness, she who craves power deems who returns and who does not. And she is greedy."

"Stone," he murmured. "My name is Stone."

My throat went tight as his gaze ran over my features, and I wondered then what he might be seeing, because he didn't ask how I knew these things. Instead, he dropped to one knee beside the bale as though he planned to pull a blade from beneath it. I tensed, every fibre alert for sudden movement.

But he only narrowed his gaze at me. "Which of those fates had you planned for me, then, I wonder?"

My mouth dropped open at the sudden shift in topic, but I snapped it shut.

"I know you are loathe to name the purveyor of my assassination," he went on. "And I imagine there is some blood vow that holds your tongue even if you wanted to save yourself from my wrath. But this I do offer you. I won't work it out of you so long as you do a favor for me in return."

"A favor?"

He nodded. "A small one. You see, I cannot deliver these women to the tavern, nor can I send them home to their realm. Not now. They are far too broken to live in the mortal world and not put ours in danger."

I swallowed, doing my best not to look over his shoulder at the women. I knew what he was going to ask before he spoke the words, and yet, I still wasn't prepared for the grief in the words.

The air between us went still, as if the darkness had just sucked in a breath.

"I want you to kill them for me."

Chapter 5

FOR A HEARTBEAT, I thought I'd misheard him. The fire crackled between us, its light drawing out the planes of his face, the tired curve of his mouth—too calm for the words that chilled the air between us. I couldn't decide what bothered me more: his command or the quiet plea beneath it.

"Kill them?" The words sank into me, slow and heavy, until the meaning turned the stew in my stomach to gravel. I could almost hear Aiofe's laughter in the dark, low and knowing, and my voice came out thinner than I meant.

His hand planted itself on my knee, warm and heavy. "Surely you have no compunction in taking a few mortal lives if you were willing to take a single fae one."

"I've not been paid to do such service."

His head canted to the side knowingly. "Haven't you?" His hand squeezed. Hard.

I got the message. I'd already been paid. I was alive.

Setting the bowl on the floor of the stable, I rose to my feet, the warmth of his touch still lingering. He looked up at me, and in that moment, I knew I could draw my blade without being questioned. I hadn't truly expected this ease. I'd thought to plead ignorance and vulnerability, let him think he'd given me succor, when all along I was a serpent in his path, quietly nesting in his hair as he passed by blind to me.

But here. Here was a chance to finish what I'd started. To claim my bounty from the queen.

"You won't ask me the name?" I asked quietly.

"I don't need to hear it," he said from below me. "That vow is yours to keep."

A strange taste moved over my palate, a scent of buttery sweetness so strange it coated my palate and made my cheeks fill with pleasure. I blinked at him, trying to understand where it was coming from even though I knew it was mingled with his own perspiration.

Beyond the broad door of the stable, the women had already given up standing in a huddle, even though they were careful to stay out of the light between the barn and the tavern.

Irina was staring up at the rafters, perhaps looking for her bed. She looked tired. The darkness of the evening hollowed out her tear troughs and circled the crest of each socket. No one else would notice the sickly pallor of her skin here in the dark, but I saw it. I saw too, the scars on her arms as she hugged herself in the threadbare linen shift.

Even so, there was a grace to her posture, a determination. She wanted to live. She would cling to breath the way her skin clung to her bones, sticking like glue to the knobby parts and refusing to be scraped free.

"They trust you," I said, my hand going to my blade on my hip.

"And I can't break that," he said, shifting just enough to block the mortals' view of my weapon as I slid it free of its sheath.

I lifted my chin. The pressure that had been building inside me let go with a whoosh of air. Everything in the air clenched like a fist.

"Then you're a coward," I said.

I jerked my hand upward and sideways, slicing perfectly, expertly beneath his upraised chin. It wasn't as neat as I'd hoped. He saw the movement and reacted, but it wasn't soon enough, no matter how fast he was.

He thought me a pathetic novice, and had lowered his guard accordingly. Just as I'd expected when he'd foolishly invited me into his camp to warm myself by his fire.

"Bleed out your pity for those poor wretches," I said as I looked down at his body, already slumping to the side of the hay bale. Bright crimson blood had begun to seep from his neck, his hand clamped over his throat to stem the tide.

The women screamed as one.

I kicked at the bits of hay on the floor.

"These humans won't grieve the race who enslaved them or thank the male who ordered their pity deaths. Your compassion is wasted."

The horse snorted and blew hair at me from its stall and then let go one long, keening note that sounded so un-equine that I couldn't help casting a bewildered look over my shoulder to see what had made it.

It was a mistake, of course. A stupid one. The horse was gone when I scanned the stall, and confused, I turned in a slow circle, scanning for the beast.

As I did so, I caught the onslaught of thunderous and frantic steps pounding earth and wood.

In the instant of peripheral vision, I caught the women's reaction. They were running to the slumped-over Stone, coming for me.

I pivoted too late, looking for the horse, thinking the women a non-threat as they tried in vain to save their benefactor.

Except only one of them skidded to her knees beside him. The others thrust pitchforks at me.

Back-stepping, I slammed into something solid. And massive.

Whatever it was, it loomed up behind me and created a bank of sinewy muscle that caged me against an immovable force. The stink of blood and manure and something far muskier circled the air, pricking my nostrils.

That miasma of overstimulation paralyzed me, making me forget how to gather my magics around me and disappear into the shadow lands or even straddle the lines of worlds.

In the next second, a fat, stinking hand clamped down over my mouth and nostrils. Another, python like arm wrapped around my midsection, holding me fast.

The women froze too. The terror in their eyes led a line higher than my head even as they dropped their weapons and ran.

I dared one glance upward, but all I could see of whatever stood above me, holding me tight in its grip, were nostrils so large they reminded me of a Clydesdale's.

A fae of sorts. Not high fae. Some sort of low-base creature with magic to shapeshift, I guessed, from equine to fae form. I'd never seen a horse shifter, but it explained the disappearance of Stone's mount.

With the suffocating hand cutting off my breath, and the other holding me fast, I tried to plead with my gaze, hoping that even if I couldn't see its face, he could see mine.

It was a vow. Hadn't he heard that? A blood vow, one I couldn't break. Had he no sisters, no loved ones that he would kill for?

But all of that was silent and wordless, and the creature couldn't read my thoughts, only my deeds. It shifted, pulling me back further into the stable and slamming my chest into a stall door. His forearms took most of the hit, but I had the feeling he didn't care. Rather than let me go, his grip tightened on my mouth, forcing my lips into my teeth. I tasted blood.

For a second, I thought I'd somehow managed to call to my magic, because the edges of my vision started to go black. It was the prickling behind my ears, popping little bubbles in the spaces of my sinuses, that told me the truth.

I was suffocating. And if I was unsure that was happening, the words he growled out as he spun around and braced his back against the stall door, his feet planted so far in front of him that I was all but laying on his thighs, gave me the truth.

"You die now," it said.

MY SISTER DIED WITH a curse on her breath.

She'd lived a century before I was born to the Nocturnes, and with her unique magics of seeing hidden truths of time and beyond, she served as our most revered oracle until the moment an angel stole that last breath, swallowing the curse that coated her tongue before she could release it.

Powerful and revered as she was, she was never the Sacred Seer to me. Enyali was my true sister. My elder by a century, she guided me, taught me to be who I was, and how to gather and use my magic. She helped me understand it.

And when I bemoaned the need to touch down in the Nocturnes to keep it recharged, she explained how lucky we in the Nocturnes were that the source of our power was our home realm and not some ephemeral thing that others could steal.

That was our natal magic, something most fae gained from a parent. But the darkness was our great mother, and she gifted us all with part of her power. That natal magic kept us grounded. We could always find enough power in the darkness to heal and recharge when we began to waste.

It was why the sisters of the Nocturnes rarely ended in Aiofe's dungeons. We had our own source, a magic that could always be claimed simply by returning home.

That, my sister said, was the true power of our magic. She believed it so adamantly that she died for it.

But while Enyali's natal magic kept her strong, and her innate magics gave her a seer's prescience in sight, mine was more unique.

No other sister of the Nocturnes could see equally well in both the light and in the dark. Deepest dark held no secrets from me. Even in the pitch black of the Nocturnes, where my sisters had lived for centuries, I was an anomaly.

In the gloom of an Earthbound night, I saw every wound on my sister's body as she lay dying. The piercing, gaping wounds where holy light shone through to the pavement were so bright I had to turn away in pain as that bastard split a seam of light down her heart center.

She didn't cry out, though I felt her agony in my marrow. As sisters in the Nocturnes, where every fae was kin to another, Enyali and I were connected through blood and magic. In that moment, I felt her death, and I heard her curse, and though I tried to save her, it was the only moment she let that sacred calling come between us.

I teetered in that space now as the beast held me in its grasp, and I almost spilled over into death with her as I straddled the ley line of the realms of darkness and light that made up my magic. The moment cursed me with the clarity of memory, a horror I'd buried long ago but that sliced up through the earth I'd packed it into.

My own words echoed in my mind as I'd begged her to let me execute the bastard who had shot her through with the horror of white, god-sourced light.

"It is done," she whispered as I lay over her body, crooked and broken upon the earthen floor of a primitive, man-made temple. The megalithic stones rose above us in a circle, drawing energy from the earth to call to their master, and getting an angel instead.

I draped myself over her chest, trying to pull the light from her body and absorb it into the shadows of my magic. My hands were wet as I reached for her cheeks, trying to color life back into them, but only managed to smear my own blood over her face.

"It's not done," I growled, my gaze training on the beads of water that kept falling onto my skin from somewhere above me. "It can't be done. This isn't the way you go, Enyali."

"Who says?" She rasped and then laughed as though she'd just made some off-color joke. "Are you the Nocturne's seer, now, Ruby?"

"The Morvannons of the Nocturnes do not die this way, Enyali. They go in rage and violence. They don't just accept death." My throat choked on each word, making them come out in tight ribbons of syllables.

She managed to lift her hand long enough to run her fingers along mine as they rested on her cheek.

"Don't cry, sister," she said.

I shook my head, indignant. I wasn't crying. I didn't even know what weeping was. Her smile was wan, pulling pale lips over increasingly pale skin.

"I've seen you," she said. "This moment is for you, sister. Don't take that from me."

She clenched my fingers in a spasm so tight I winced. "He will know you, Ruby. Remember that. He will know the truth of you and he will break his own vow to claim you."

"Who, Enyali?" I fought to lift her into my arms, but she fought as much as I did, and I had to content myself with laying her on my lap. "What is all this for that you would sacrifice your life force to an angel? We don't need his magic that much. The Nocturnes will go on without his power, but it can't thrive without yours."

Her lips parted just as a shadow fell over me, swallowing the last of her form into darkness, and I felt her go. Everything inside me wound itself up in the same way a twisted thread bunched and looped and bucked at the assault on its form when twirled too tight.

And I found myself on my hands and knees, bowed before an energy so vast and greedy for power, I couldn't hold myself up anymore. I went flat, like a worm, my belly inching along the hard pack of earth. This wasn't the earthen realm. It wasn't the Nocturnes. It was the whole of the Stygian Darkness and its queen's own soul.

I fully expected to find myself inching through the pitch of the Stygian Darkness by my nails as I sought Enyali's energy in the dungeons of Aiofe's throne room. I prayed for it. The angel's life ended in a scream as its light banked out, and I filled it with my own darkness, losing myself to the pleasure of feeling my magic drain into him and hollow him out.

I reveled in the knowledge that I had earned my wasting, that I would feel the same darkness as Enyali in the throne room of Kumara.

The memory fractured. The scent of earth and angels burned away, replaced by the stench of wood smoke and iron. Pain anchored me back into flesh—into a body that wasn't dead after all.

Hateful light bled through my eyelids in a soft pinkish glow, haloed above my head when I peeled them open just enough to realize I was not in the dungeons at all.

Walls of smoke-darkened oak met my gaze. A window, covered in hand-hewn shutters, half-opened to reveal lead glass that mottled the view of the pastures beyond. At my feet, the blacksteel knobs of an ornate bedpost were draped with blood-stained linen strips, so many that it looked like whoever had done the bleeding had to be dead.

I just knew it wasn't me. And I groaned out loud to discover it.

"Holy Morrigan," said a female voice, startling me enough to let go of a rapid-fire series of curses that ended with a squeak coming from the voice and a rustling of fabric as she retreated.

A door slammed. The jarring of it hurt my head. Or maybe my head just hurt anyway, and the door slamming was just the catalyst that made me realize the pain existed.

I couldn't even roll my head toward the sound of the noise. Just lifting tentative fingers to my head seemed a Herculean effort. My hands might as well have been encased in petrified wood.

But I made the effort, feeling as though my arms didn't belong to me as I applied a testing, tentative touch to the throbbing just behind my right ear, where the worst of the pain pulsed like a blood-bloated spider curled in the center of its web.

"Fuck," I said when the awkward move resulted in me whacking the wound straight on. I did manage to move my head then, and dizziness swam over my vision. My stomach curdled. Leaning to the side in case I vomited,

I cradled my body around the blankets. Because there were blankets, thankfully. My bare skin was cocooned in soft linen.

After several seconds, once the vertigo subsided, I was better able to assess the damage.

It felt more like the hard knob of a burled oak than the poisoned abdomen of a fae spider. I winced at the softest of touches, and probed around the base of it, tracing out the lines of pain to see how far the injury went. At least the worst of it seemed contained to that one spot.

Nothing I couldn't handle if I was careful. And knowing the damage was critical to the next steps of assessing exactly where I was. Whether I could get out. Whether I needed to.

Using my hands propped at my sides, I heaved myself upright. Nausea threatened again, but I bit it back. This wasn't the Nocturnes, and it wasn't Aiofe's Darkness. That meant I was far from safe even if I was lying in a soft bed beneath buttery linen.

Morning. That was the first thought that came to mind. Not a terrible thing, but definitely confusing. Something told me it should be nighttime.

The second was that I was in a tavern, and that too threw me off. I wasn't sure why I was there or how I'd arrived. Noises from below filtered up through the floorboards. Rutting sounds from the room next door suggested the sort of rutting that occurred between a patron and a prostitute. I was sure I heard the distinct sound of whinnying.

And that horse-like sound slammed realization into my soggy brain.

I remembered the moments that had brought me to the upper realms of daylight. A vow to my queen. Days of trailing a powerful fae. Cutting his throat and being caught in the brutal embrace of his mount, who was evidently a horse shifter currently enjoying the embraces of a prostitute next door.

"So you're a shadow shifter," said a gruff voice from across the room. I startled, the motion making me wince as my head reminded me how much it hurt.

A creaking sound caught my ear long before I could turn to the sound of Stone's voice, and I knew it was too late to even try leaping out of the bed. I sank back down onto my back, my hands working at the sheets in case I could grab enough to wrap around his throat if he got too close.

"I thought I killed you," I said.

A throaty chuckle. "Oh, you nearly did. But for Nutkin, and the women risking their own lives to get help, I'd be lending current to a bird's wing right now."

"Feeding Aiofe's darkness more like," I muttered and scooted sideways as he prowled from the side of the fireplace where I'd not noticed him because he'd been covered over by a hefty-looking fur that he'd tossed to the floor when he'd risen.

He halted beside the bed and looked down at me. That penetrating gaze was nothing compared to the power evident in his naked chest. I hadn't meant to say anything, let alone let slip Aiofe's name out, but thankfully, he seemed more interested in figuring out how vulnerable I was as he stood there, clad in soft-looking baggy linen trousers.

Despite the rumpled look of those trousers, and the bags beneath his eyes, even half-dressed and wounded, he looked more dangerous than he had in armor.

A crisp white bandage ringed his throat just beneath his chin. Seeing it, I realized how clumsy my strike had been. I'd missed the carotid, no doubt, and probably just cut into the small pouch of skin beneath his jaw. I sighed heavily, and his fingers went to the bandage in echo of the way I traced it with my eyes.

I had been incredibly lucky I'd got a shot in at all, and I knew it.

My eyes stopped at the thickest part of the bandage, a place sporting a rusty-looking stain. The tips of his hair sported the same, coppery shade. I imagined him running his blood-covered fingers over the ends.

"Blade is a healer of sorts," he said, dropping his hand to his sides. "Says in a century the scar will be invisible."

I grunted and slid a leg free on the other side of the bed, an automatic move borne of a well-ingrained, lifetime habit for self-preservation.

"Don't move," he growled, and the pure rage in the tone froze me in place despite myself. With one leg hanging down toward the floor, barely touching the wooden slats, I was uncomfortable and vulnerable, but I didn't dare argue. Not with that voice.

Instead, I gripped the sheets, tugging at them beneath the blanket. Fuel if he came at me, flimsy as it might be. I wasn't sure I could gather enough magic to slide into the underworld realm or even if there was enough magic in the vicinity to allow it. So I hedged.

"Like you weren't already planning to kill me," I said, managing to free about an inch of material and bunch it into my palm. "You even admitted it would be in your own damn time. Don't be surprised that I decided to preempt your plans."

He crossed his arms over his chest, and the muscles tensed in time with the muscle tightening in his jaw. "I might kill you now," he said. "Choke you with that sheet you're yanking on."

His eyes narrowed before they flickered toward the wall where the rutting noises had gone eerily quiet. "Or maybe I'll pass you over to Nutkin first. I have a feeling the human woman they gave him was woefully inadequate for his frustrations."

The memory of those thick arms wrapped around me, of the stink of manure, and the strange coarseness of his hair lit a fire of panic in my belly. Of all the things in this magical world, the thought of intimacy terrified me the most. But a straight-out assault?

"I'd kill him first."

He laughed. "You couldn't even kill me proper. Oh, Nightling," he said in a mocking echo of the term I'd called him. "You have no idea what you'd be up against. Have you heard of Nutkin's race? Low based fae who keep certain aspects of their size and shape when they transform to fae form." He winked evilly. "You saw the size of the horse that carried me."

I swallowed. Yes, I had. I'd trailed along behind for days as the mount carried two of them at a time, never seeming to tire even beneath the burden of blankets and packs. Standing higher than any normal fae mount by at least several hands, I wasn't even sure it wasn't some abomination created by a master creator.

Calling it a horse was a kindness. It was a beast at best. I pulled my hands, both of them, out from beneath the sheets and laid them on top of the blankets.

"If you were going to straight out murder me, you would have done so by now, not had me repaired and put to bed like a babe."

"Repaired?" He snuffed too loudly through his nose. "I did nothing of the sort. Nutkin suffocated the life out of you till you fell and hit your head on the salt lick. The stable hand brought you here because he realized you were still breathing and thought I would like to dispatch you myself."

A soft sigh fled my lungs. I guess that explained why he had a bandage and I didn't. My hand strayed to my head again, touching down on the huge walnut behind my ear.

"So why not smother me in my sleep?"

He dropped a foot onto the mattress, propping his arm on his knee as he regarded me.

"I wanted you to know when I took your life," he said in a voice that held no sympathy. "I wanted you to really see me. And there was no other place to put you except my room while I was being tended to."

I eyeballed the size of the calf near my chest, the large boot leaving a stain on the crisp sheets.

"And now?" I asked, squinting at him. "Why not do it while I'm lying helpless?" I traced the line of muscle all the way up to the face leaning toward me and held that implacable gaze, knowing my own expression was as deadpan as his. "You've got me where you want me. Easy prey."

"Do I?" he asked, nudging his toe toward my leg. He moved it easily despite my resistance. "I've watched you disappear and reappear several times these last days" His arm left the prop of his knee so he could tangle his fingers in my hair. "Black as the shadows you shift into."

He canted his head as he tugged, not playfully, but not viciously either.

Even so, my eyes watered.

"I'm not a shadow shifter," I said.

One more pull, this time harder, as though testing the truth of my words. "The first piece of actual truth you've offered me."

"Is it not in any fae to lie," I hedged with a statement of fact.

He snorted and released my hair to tap my forehead. "You lie like any good fae," he said. "In half truths and shadows. But my question is why. Who are you protecting?"

"I told you."

"Your sister," he said, dropping his foot to the floor and sitting on the side of the bed. It dipped down with his weight, dragging me closer to him. "That's who you're protecting but not who hired you, the one who is threatening your sister. I want her name, Nightling."

He planted both hands beneath my skull, and leveraged my chin upward, exposing my throat as he leaned toward me. "You smell of cinnamon and cloves," he said, his nostrils inhaling, his mouth very close to my pulse. For a moment, I thought he would sink those canines into my flesh, and I held my breath, squeezing my eyes shut as I willed my magics closer.

"I didn't smell it in the stables or in the bushes, but it's distinct here in this room where only my own scents carry."

His fingers dug behind my ears, hard enough to make me wince. He wasn't going to tear my throat out with his teeth. No, he was going to dig straight into my skull with those powerful fingers of his and scoop out any living matter. I had a horrid image of him feasting on the tissues and licking his lips.

He shook my head hard enough that it rattled. "You think I don't know that pheromone?"

"You're mad," I yelled, struggling now no matter how much it hurt. "Let me go. Let go or I'll slit your belly open."

He might have laughed at that; I wasn't sure. Because in an instant I was hauled out of bed by my ears. I hung from his hands, eyes level with his, my feet dangling for an entire ten seconds.

My lip curled back as I found an ounce of strength. I snapped my knee up and caught him square between the legs.

The pain that shot across his face put a smile on mine. It was a lucky shot, and though I had enough space to wind my leg back and aim my knee again, whatever pain he felt didn't prevent him from slamming me up against the wall and pinning my legs between his thighs.

Powerful. That thought was the only one that went screaming through my mind. He was as strong as Aiofe had said.

My lungs seized on the last ounce of air within them. Mouth agape like a fish as I fought for oxygen, I was aware that his face, gorgeous and perfectly cut, had turned ugly with rage.

He slammed me against the wall hard enough to rattle the boards. His body pressed against mine in an intimate way that only violence can offer. Something inside me cracked open. I expected those hands to begin roaming my body, to find secret places as his mouth dropped onto mine and forced itself on me.

I closed my eyes, preparing for it, going slack with cell memory, every inch of my body, shadow and shape surrendering out of long buried fear.

"Look at me," he growled and shook me harder. Roughly enough that my teeth bit down on my tongue.

"Look at me because I swear to the Holy Morrigan that I will kill you one way or the other, but if blind, it will be more painful."

I forced my eyes open, letting the hate I felt show on my face.

"Joke's on you, Dayling," I said through the taste of blood. "I'm already dead."

Chapter 7

NO ONE IN THE Nocturnes or any other corner of the Stygian Darkness was truly alive in the way most fae would understand it. Certainly not in the way the fae of the light worlds were. My peculiar state of magic was such that I could straddle the lines of the worlds. But unlike within Aiofe's court, pockets of the Darkness were more alive than wasted.

Fae from the Nocturnes were a blend of wasted energy and fae magic. In my youth, I could shift into a falcon or an owl and find the worlds of light, taking to their skies for a short while, long enough to hear the crispness of the clean air, taste the breeze as it lofted me through the trees. If the magic was strong, or the wind was right, I could take the shape of a high fae for a few delicate moments.

The Nocturnes gave to every fae in her season the ability to hold form in the day worlds. Like dandelion seeds on the wind, we were cast forth to find fertile ground to gather for the gardens of the mother world.

I'd collected much during my long life. Enyali, as a seer, could peer through the shadows to find the right soils, and we'd bring them back to till beneath our darkness, watering the magic with blood.

It was the boy who had broken that joy for me. His wonder and eagerness to enjoy the caresses of the Sidhe who all but smothered him with the cloying magics of the underworld was painful.

"Him," Enyali had told me. "He's yours."

The moment I'd bid for him, I'd also caught the look of sadness on her face, as though I'd committed to some path I couldn't see in the underbrush, trusting her to guide me.

Now, I looked at Stone as he held me aloft, and I watched his expression mirror that look for an instant before it moved to rage and then confusion and finally, to a mastered mask of deadpan neutrality.

He dropped me onto the floor and took a step backward.

"Aiofe's minion," he muttered. His nostrils flared and softened, a breath of my scent charging the air. "You're from the Darkness. That's why you are phasing in and out."

I resisted the urge to rub the pain from the back of my head and scalp. "I am of no world and all worlds," I said. "Never fully whole. But I am not a minion for the queen. Not the way you think."

"You smell of her." His mouth curled back from his teeth.

His words weren't a confession, just a distraction that pinched his eyebrows together, but my mouth twitched just the same. "Spoken like a fae who has met her."

"If you'd done your research," he said, "you would know the breadth of my knowledge in relation to your queen."

That rankled, even though I'd done what I could to foster the notion that I was an inept novice, because research was something I didn't leave to chance.

But it didn't matter, because he seemed uninterested in my reaction and more interested in his own suppositions and began to pace back and forth in front of me.

"It is she who has your sister," he guessed, and when I didn't deny or agree, he jabbed at my chest with a rigid finger. "I know how Aiofe works, and though it took me a ludicrous amount of time to figure it out, I know I'm right."

His gaze was a challenge. I ignored it. If he were going to kill me, I'd take the rest of it with me to the Darkness.

Exasperated at my silence, he prowled the room, his boots making too much noise every time he took a heavy step, as though he wanted me to pay attention to each footfall.

"Aiofe birthed my older brother, Blade," he said, idly pulling a book from a bookcase and holding it open. Running a finger down the center of the inside of the spine, he didn't bother to look up as he continued, each word like bits of glass being ground into my skin. "She had access to a suite in my father's manse, so I know her well. She treated me like a son when my own mother was unable."

His voice broke on that last, and my shoulder blades pinched together, alert, the predator in me paying attention.

I thought about that, about the queen I knew treating a creature of any sort with kindness, and found it difficult to imagine.

"I too, have a mentor like that," I said as I looked past him to the shadows gathering in the corners. The firelight seemed less bright. A chill ran over my skin.

"The Madre. We in the Nocturnes are all her daughters though not from her body."

Something in my voice must have caught his attention because he canted his head at me and the shadows fled, replaced by the sounds of screaming and rutting and finally, of someone sobbing in plea for his life.

"You hate her," he said.

I blinked, clearing the creep of memory from my sight.

He inched toward me the way a rabbit might advance on a wolf that has laid its head on its paws.

"Maybe not whole," he said in a soft voice, looking at me with something akin to compassion. "But not entirely broken."

Air fled my lungs in a soft gasp. My head bobbed backward, and I fought for equilibrium.

For a moment, the room swam with shadows, and I knew my magic was claiming me.

This time against my will, uncalled, as though to disprove his words or to prove to me what I'd known all along. That I was broken, no matter what he believed. I wanted his words to be true so badly, I fought to hold on to my space in the world of light.

There in the tavern, with the lights flickering and shadows crawling along the stones of the fireplace like an army of ants coming for me, I sucked in a breath. I held on to the magic of Stone's energy, the room he stood in, the sound of the flames eating themselves alive so they could grow higher.

Because I wasn't ready to go. I didn't want to leave. I didn't want the magic of the source, didn't want its suffusing possession as it gave to me another charge of power. If this moment would be my last, I thought I could go to Aiofe's dungeons satisfied.

I was not broken. My nature was as it should be. All those years of Enyali insisting it was so, those centuries I wouldn't believe, her, I knew it then as it came from his mouth. I believed it.

For an instant, despite his sense of rage and betrayal, maybe even because of it, he had seen me.

But it wasn't enough to hold me there. I felt myself evaporating into the darkness. My weapons lay on the chair. Stone stood half a dozen paces away.

I might have time to grab for one thing before I lost control and returned to the world of darkness and shadow.

So I made a choice. My only choice.

Before my limbs lost all corporeality to the shadows, I lunged.

He was fast. His was a battle-trained swiftness, borne of centuries of fighting and training and living through it all. So I wasn't sure he would even be in the same spot when I reached it. I just went, with Enyali's voice echoing in my head. "He'll know you."

The moment my arms went around his waist, I knew an all-encompassing and searing pain. I almost let go, and might have except for the whisper of her voice in the back of my head, and the sensation that if I just held on everything would be alright.

I was vaguely aware that the pain was likely his own magic fighting against mine. Light against dark. Revelation in the face of secrets. A piercing sort of exultation, like stepping into the day after years of black solitude.

But as bright and relieving as light magic could be, shadow magic such as mine was all-encompassing. One second of darkness carried the weight of confusion and terror. It was magic I'd hated for as long as I'd lived. I envied the high fae with their glittering skin and ease of life because their magics were innate, part of them.

It was in their blood and tissues, and they didn't need to touch ground in their own realm just to keep from wasting.

They were whole as they were.

So he succumbed as I expected because he didn't have time to respond, and when he did, it was with utter bewilderment as my darkness sealed him off from his world and chipped away at his beautiful fae body until it was nothing but magic and molecules.

He succumbed, and I held on. Light shattered into black shards. The air turned solid in my lungs, and when it thinned again, we were somewhere else. An earthy musk clung to the air. A damp chill shivered over my skin. Beside me, Stone's breath came harsh and uneven, a sound too fragile for this place.

The Nocturnes. A home I'd not been allowed to wander freely within for decades.

Despite my not walking the damp soil in the Nocturnes, of not smelling the night lilies blooming under a full moon, I knew I'd unerringly landed in the only place my ley lines would take me without triggering the banishment spell and sizzling my hide into a dozen pieces of roasted char.

The broad copper door of the temple where Enyali spent so many of her days held a sliver of sanctuary magic, cast there by the oracle herself, letting me and Stone phase in effortlessly. I doubted any of the sisters even knew it existed.

But I did, and while I'd honored my exile except for the few moments it took to recharge my magic, since the moment The Madre had decreed it, I came now because it was the only play I had left.

Uncloaked. In view of the entire clan. Because I didn't have enough magic in me to shadow Stone too.

The darkness was so absolute, I knew Stone couldn't see me or anything else. Even if his vision adjusted, without the torches lit, and in the waned phase of the moon, there was little light to adjust to.

But I could see him. In the darkness, he was a glittering, gorgeous thing, standing out against the blackness like a coin glinting at the bottom of a well.

I stumbled backward against the door, almost stumbling to my knees from the sudden release of magic. My chest heaved with each heavy breath that razored through my lungs. Everything around me came into focus as I leaned on my thighs.

The thatched stone roundhouses. The well with its wooden bucket and hemp rope. Magic winked at me from gaps in the thatch and mud where inside, the fae females of the clan used their powers for whatever task or pleasure they were set to.

To my right lay the Sidhe version of the River Styx, its viscous black eddy relieved now and again by a burst of magic from below as it echoed the strokes of Charon's oar on the other side of the world.

Wafts of sulfur crept along the ground like fog. Swamp-colored mist swirled about my feet. I felt a tug from the realm I'd left, Stone's world, as the magic settled, but it let go the way it always did—shutting off like a door being slammed closed.

Stone felt it too, I know. He stood very still for a long moment, blinking frantically as though to force his vision to adjust. I felt a pang for him, knowing his blindness probably scared him. And when the telltale and familiar sounds of clicking and snapping began to echo off the buildings around the square, he swung around, flailing at each noise.

Confusion and wariness etched his gorgeous face into something I knew would bother him if he could see it for himself, but fear is such a primal thing, there was no shame in it. I hoped he'd understand that.

Behind me, the copper door nestled into the front of the black-stone temple where Enyali spent so many of her days. Weeping Ivy clung to its facade in wispy, anemic tendrils. In the light, the leaves would be scarlet, but here in the darkness, they were just another shade of gray.

I didn't need to open the door to know the altar that dominated the space was bare of offerings, the candles unlit. The pool of water rippling in a large obsidian bowl at the foot of Enyali's gilded chair would reflect nothing but the crystal-studded ceiling above and the sacred circle in the middle designed to filter in starlight and the errant capture of light magic.

No predictions waited while the oracle was absent. The basin was nothing but an ordinary bowl of water. Who even knew if the sisters had kept it filled or if it had dried up in the century since I'd been inside last.

The Nocturnes were barren of that kind of magic now that the seer was gone. The Morvannon line had never seeded another oracle. Only I was left. Ruby Morvannon of the Nocturnes. Half-dweller. A traitor to the long line, who did the unconscionable thing of selling her magics in service to others. An excommunicated Sidhe who owned no home.

It had been a year since I'd stayed longer than it took to recharge my magic, and never in the village square. Always, always in this tiny sliver of grace Enyali had left me. It occurred to me for the first time as I stood in the safety of that space that she'd likely known I'd need this small sanctuary after she was gone.

"What is this place?" Stone whispered. A plume of mist lifted, showing his boots had moved a pace or two. "Where am I?"

"The Nocturnes," I said, keeping my voice low. I knew he couldn't see me, and I wasn't about to give away my location so he could jump me. We didn't need that sort of tussle on the steps of the temple, and certainly not within hearing of the clan.

"You'd be smart to stay quiet."

I backed up a step, leaving him blinking as he tried to adjust.

I'd never dared caretake Enyali's space inside. I didn't want to see her scrying basin empty or the plants she nurtured dried to dust or gone to the earth that sustained them.

But what I was about to do right then meant I'd have to step outside that safe space for the first time since she'd died. And the first thing I intended was to pay homage to the long-lost oracle, knowing that to step outside the protected area was to bring down the magics of exile and banishment upon me.

That one movement, so simple, was all it took. I felt the awful burning beneath my solar plexus that indicated the exile magic had been triggered. It was enough to steal my breath, leave me heaving as I fought to fuel my lungs.

And then, as if on cue, several sharp clicking noises echoed through the air and bounced off the surrounding buildings. They cut through the darkness, each of a unique pitch as familiar to me as my own breath.

"What's happening?" Stone said, and a note of uncertainty pooled into his voice, an unbidden thing that I knew by the way he winced, made him feel shame. "What's that unholy noise?"

His hands flew to his ears, blocking out the din, and my gaze trailed to the forms coming out of the roundhouse, streaming out of the hills beyond, the cellars dug into the earth to store vegetables and oils and wine.

But I was too caught up in the pain to answer. Hunched over, hands on my knees, I struggled to fight back the searing agony burning its way through every layer of skin. Beads of sweat trailed down my back as I hitched in quick breaths that were nowhere near large enough to keep me on my feet.

Bowing beneath it all, I couldn't help lurching toward him and that space that I knew could cut the pain. I'd been a fool to think I could bear it in the first place.

Even before I stepped into the zone, I knew I was too late.

"Ruby Morvannon."

The voice calling to me was nearly drowned out by the clicks and clacks and piercing sounds of radar as the sisters assembled, but I heard it just the same. I doubted whether Stone understood the biting tone of the syllables to be language amid the other myriad sounds almost too high-pitched for the normal fae ear to bear. But I heard it. And I knew immediately who had called out to me.

The pain stopped, leaving me trembling and drenched in sweat. And I gulped in air as if it were water. There was no doubt in my mind why the magics were lifted.

Rubbing my arms, I angled myself toward the voice, grateful for the respite. The Madre emerged from the maw of shadows to the east, the roundhouse behind her, outlining her shape by the firelight within. Her warriors flanked her like shadows stitched to the air.

She stood there, the Madre, surrounded by her caste of warriors, and I could see them all turning their gazes away from me and toward the massive fae male standing with me on the threshold of the temple.

My knees still shook as I staggered toward him, thinking only that I had to get to him before they knew he was there, before they claimed him.

I leapt for him, pulling his hands away from his ears as soon as I got close enough to touch him. It was a risk getting close enough to him for him to strike out at me, but I bet on his near blindness to keep me safe.

"You're with me, Stone of Terran from the Shadow Court," I rasped out. "Remember that."

He pivoted sharply to the sound of my voice, wincing as the last of the noises died away and he caught my order. I back-stepped, moving to a place just below the top step, Stone a few feet ahead on the threshold between me and the shadows gathering at the square's edge.

Even though he knew it was me speaking, I could tell he was still straining to see through the dark, to get his bearings. As if by some miracle, his gaze pinned itself exactly to mine, and I sagged at the recognition in his face. For a breath, I forgot the danger. I forgot everything except the fact that he'd seen me, even here in the shadows.

"You'll adjust to the darkness," I whispered. "Give it time."

And that was all the time I had to warn him. The Madre, the eldest of the Nocturnes, extricated herself from the throng. She who carved out this place in the darkness for us to exist, she who had banished me from it, who knew I could see her as clearly as if there was full sunlight illuminating her every frail bone, stepped away from the protection of her warriors and faced me.

"You must want to die," she said in that raspy voice.

Several of the Morrakai closed in. Silent. Like a blink in the darkness. And yet Stone sensed it. He tensed. Nostrils flared.

"You're with me," I said again and almost reached out to calm him. The energy coming off him in waves was not panicked, but it was panicking. One wrong move and he might do something foolish.

"Is that supposed to calm me?" he asked, voice filled with suppressed annoyance.

"It's supposed to warn you," I barked out, and Sevina's head tilted up at the threat in my voice.

"You brought a male into our midst," she said. "You must want to suffer a painful death."

"I have honored your decree all these decades," I called out, not quite brave enough to step off the steps of the temple. I might slide back into shadow at any moment, but Stone hadn't moved. I needed to be in range if things went south. "Aren't you the least bit curious to know why I return on pain of immediate execution?"

Stone sucked in a breath at the comment. "I'm with you, am I?" he ground out. "Thanks for that."

Sevina shrugged, ignoring Stone's comment, her papery shoulders making a rustling sound beneath her dyed flax-woven linen. "You have returned dozens of times despite the decree," she sniffed. "You think I don't know each time you touch sacred earth?"

"Then I suppose I should thank you for not executing me dozens of times over, Sevina," I said, sketching a stiff bow. Her name was reserved for those most intimate to her, but since she'd exiled me and I was no longer truly of the Nocturnes, I refused to call her by the title due her.

She sniffed at the lack of respect. "Perhaps it was more about making sure we didn't obliterate the sanctity of the temple."

At that, she signaled over her shoulder. And in a rush, the sisters came at us.

Chapter 8

THE TEMPLE STEPS SHUDDERED under the onslaught before I saw them—a swarm of sisters, dark shapes cutting through thicker dark as the sisters launched themselves at the temple steps.

I knew Stone couldn't see them coming, but it was obvious he felt the energy, heard the rush of feet as they stormed their way toward us.

Effortlessly, as though he could intuit their direction and intention, he neatly side-stepped the threat. He shifted with predator grace, back hitting the temple wall, arms splayed out along its surface. The move wasn't retreat; it was cunning reconnaissance. That battle instinct drove him to the temple door, but it left me, perhaps unintentionally, open to attack.

Not that it mattered. My sisters had middling vision in the dark, but mine was absolute. In heartbeats, I assessed the distance, the speed, and exactly who would meet me first.

Askrid. Golden hair tied back in several braids, she outpaced the six others, her own magics in tracking putting her on an unerring path toward me.

I concentrated on her, my long-established experience at her side in battle raids offering me an insight into how she would strike. I knew she would use her spear. I knew she would try to take me from the air with a single strike to the top of my shoulder, driving the point in and using her weight to knock me off my feet.

All that information bypassed my conscious mind and went directly to my limbs and core. I didn't have time to consider Stone's welfare. All that existed in that moment was the cadre of sisters intent on my death as boots scuffed stone around me. The circle closed.

I caught a flash of braids, of steel. Then the world became elbows and knees.

Stone remained flattened against the temple, making himself part of the shadows while he assessed the terrain, the opponents as best he could with near-blind eyes.

I didn't have that luxury, but I didn't need it. I'd fought with these warriors for decades. I knew their moves.

As expected, Askrid pulled out her favorite play, leaping high into the air and using the magics gifted by her natal mother to hold her aloft like a soaring eagle for a fraction of a moment. But without the wings necessary to guide her and hold her skyward, she had to pull her spear from the sheath on her back long before she was ready. And well after I'd already pivoted and spun out of reach.

She struck me on the shoulders with her elbow, the spear missing its mark. A guttural, hateful cry tore free of her throat as I spun once more, instinctively, and thrust my forearm perfectly against her throat.

I felt the boniness of her jaw drop onto my arm as she curled inward to recover. Her breath exploded over me in a gust of air that hinted at the honeyberry wine she enjoyed in the evening.

By the time I'd yanked my arm back, drawing thrust for another punch I hoped would land on her cheek, the next sister was upon me.

I didn't know who it was. Only that her foot planted itself in my left kidney with a solid kick that stole my breath. I staggered. Askrid caught me, almost cradling me in her embrace as she dug her hands into the slight fat beneath my ribs.

"You should never have come back," she growled into my face.

I couldn't answer if I wanted to. My air was still held captive somewhere between my lungs and my throat.

Instead, I did the unthinkable out of instinct and centuries of habit. I let go of the tenuous hold I had on the realm.

The effect was immediate. I lost my sense of her arms, the smell of her breath. My feet left the cold earth of the Nocturnes, and all vision went to a blaze of unexpected light.

None of us fought with magic. Though many of the sisters possessed powers that could disengage from their bodies: water, fire, sometimes air. To do so among our own was dishonorable and earned the contempt of the entire sisterhood.

In the Nocturnes, battle amongst the cadre had always been done with muscle and sinew. Strength and speed. Decades of training and battle and raids built strength we could use in other realms when we raided.

We worked hard to gain a variety of magic. To dishonor that heritage was to earn exile.

But for me, in that moment, it wasn't about cheating. The response was a reflex, the sucking in of air after holding your breath too long. Already exiled, having spent dozens of years away from the Nocturnes, I didn't think. I reacted in a moment of self-preservation.

But that one sidestep, that straddle over two realms, cost me.

The world slammed back into focus, temple stones biting my knees as the air thickened around me again. I wasn't on the cusp of worlds anymore. The moment my feet struck Nocturne soil, the banishment spell lit through me like wildfire.

A scream ripped up my throat as I staggered beneath the sudden and unexpected pain. Askrid wasted no time in grappling me to the ground. Several more sisters pinned my legs, my arms.

I knew vaguely that my face had shifted into an owl's, that long-lost magic gifted to me by she who bore me, hooking my mouth into that of a bird of prey. With Askrid's flesh the only thing near enough my face to tear into, I dug in mercilessly, fighting against the magic of the spell, unable to kick or strike out. Rage and impotence and pain blinding me of anything except self-preservation.

But it was for nothing. Soon the searing pain of the spell was all but smothered beneath the rain of blows landing on every inch of my body. The sisters held nothing back as they attacked. All the ire and hatred and rage they'd contained for years was delivered in their blows, their kicks, and bites.

Pinned, I was nothing more than bone and skin and some shadow beneath their fury, unable to defend myself. I could see nothing but the earth beneath me. Feel nothing but pain. There were more feet stampeding their way toward me, and I knew that all two dozen of the Sisters would have a blow.

And I knew they wouldn't come with magic, because that would be too easy. Not intimate and personal enough. They wanted to feel my skin beneath their teeth, taste my blood. They wanted the sickening yield of muscle against their fists and feet.

It was the thought of that shameful deed, of imagining Enyali lost to Aiofe's dungeons, that made me go slack.

Let them take their vengeance. I deserved it. I'd been a fool to come home. I didn't belong here anymore, and the sound of more sisters coming for me was just proof of my worthlessness.

But just as I surrendered, something in the energy shifted. The smothering weight eased from my back, and the blows lessened. Someone howled in rage and pain from somewhere behind me.

I knew the sound of flesh meeting flesh in rage and violence. I knew the sounds of battle.

Lots of those sounds met my ears then, and the loudest was the sound of Stone's distinct voice as it cursed and threatened, and occasionally emitted howls of pain.

Stone had entered the battle. And from the chaos and cacophony of clicks and clacks followed by shouts of curses, I was willing to bet he was giving the sisters who had attacked me a hard time.

I cradled my ribs, preparing to get up, to move, to fight where I could, but I also heard a stampede of footsteps coming to join the fray.

And I knew there was no time even to roll over. The time to gather myself and defend was over.

I heard Stone's snarl first, then the rush of displaced air as he threw himself over me. A heartbeat later, his weight crushed the breath from my lungs.

Broad and large and long, his weight covered me from shoulder to heel. I couldn't breathe for a moment. Panic flared across my vision, momentarily blinding me.

Then I felt the enraged blows of yet more warriors raining down on him, but he didn't move or retreat. He stayed atop me, body hard and warm. Heat and iron at once, deflecting strikes where he could, and taking them in my stead when he couldn't.

"Use your magic," he rasped into my ear. "Dissolve or something."

I almost laughed at the desperation in his voice. So it had come to that, then. The two of us were not enough to hold back the fury of the Morrakai, and he'd resorted to protecting me so I could step over the ley lines into his world and take him with me.

He grunted as one of the sisters kicked him in the ribs. The soft, forced exhale from his lungs made me flinch beneath him.

"I can't," I gasped out.

"Fuck," he muttered, and in a flash of movement that shook my lungs into an inhale, he roared and flew off my back, leaving me exposed but not undefended. Instead, he took them head-on. Him, near blind and disadvantaged, but terrifying in his rage.

The noises that echoed through the square then would have sent a grown fae running for the hills.

It took everything I had in me to roll to my side. Cradling my ribs with one arm, I could just make out through the throng of frighteningly powerful female warriors, one male fighting blindly. He was something to behold. Even the warriors' expressions twisted into a sort of glee with each one he took on.

He didn't waste time aiming perfect strikes, just launched an attack at whatever shadow came for him. And they did. The Morrakai were relentless as a tsunami. Stone stood like a barrier wall, taking blow after blow, refusing to fall, giving back as much as he took.

I saw abrasions rise on his skin. Swelling ballooned beneath his eyes. When Askrid threw herself at him sideways, her right foot kicking out at his stomach, he grappled her by the ankle as though he could see her perfectly and twisted her in midair, then flung her into another warrior.

They could have used their magics against him, yet they didn't. He could have used his. He didn't.

They were as fast as he. Strong and aggressive as he was. But he was only one to their many. He couldn't stand against that tide for long.

I struggled to get to my feet. My breath was a wheeze echoed in the sound of Stone's exhales. Something had broken inside him. He couldn't win. He had to know that. But if that fact had crossed any single dendrite, he gave it no consideration.

Every fang of the Morrakai had swarmed him by then. The entire warrior caste wanted a piece of his flesh.

I managed to get to my knees, my whole body swaying. I blinked at the sight through a haze of pain. The spells pressing on me, trying to tear me apart from the inside, felt like a block of granite on my body, and shards of glass in my stomach.

And then, as though some silent signal had rung inside each of the warrior's ears, they fell back. The pressure of the banishment magic eased so gently I barely felt it disappear until I could breathe without pain.

A respite of some sort. I might have sagged in relief for it except for the pressure of the spell. Except for the way their faces were painted with glee and satisfaction. Some wore blood on their faces and arms. Some sported bites and bruises.

Stone collapsed, sliding to his backside on the temple steps. With his knees up and his hands hanging over them, he swung his gaze unerringly toward me. Though I knew I was nothing more than a shape in the darkness, his eyes found me anyway. Maybe by sound or the pull of whatever linked us now.

"What in the fuck is all this?" he asked.

Exertion frayed his normally husky voice. When he realized how tired he sounded, he pushed himself once more back onto his feet. It was clear he didn't want to look vulnerable. But I knew by the way he looked my way when he did, that he saw me clearly enough. A shape I might be in the darkness, but I was probably as hunched over as he was, the only figure who looked as badly beaten as he did.

Around us, the Morrakai spread apart as if by some silent order and took their places in double lines, barring us from the temple or the square. I watched them form this gauntlet with black humor.

"This is the Nocturnes," I said as I made my way to him, stumbling, swaying my way through the needle of space they gave me. "This is your sanctuary."

He barked out a laugh, a dark, humorless sound that echoed over the temple roof. "You have a strange way of keeping a bloke safe."

The sisters stood by. I was keenly, painfully aware of their presence, of their surveying of us as we stood there on the steps.

He leaned against the temple wall. "Why am I here? Why did you bring me?"

He didn't question why we were attacked, or why the Morrakai stood so silently by. His breath was even, but I could hear a tremor in it. Adrenaline. Not fear. I had the feeling there wasn't much he was afraid of.

"You could have let me die," I said.

His brow furrowed. A blaze of light moved through his eyes. His magic, I guessed, wanted to escape after being pent up and penned during battle. Whatever he was going to say, he would keep it to himself.

"I'm with you," he said, echoing my words back to me.

The words struck something deep, an ache that flared where his voice brushed the air between us. He deserved some truth after all that. I might truly be dead if not for him. I still couldn't understand why the Madre called off her warriors.

"Aiofe wants you dead," I whispered, daring to take one step closer to him. "I want my sister to live. This was all I could think of."

He looked off toward the Madre, where she stood conferring with her guard. "And since you failed to actually kill me in my world, you brought me here thinking to improve your odds." He rubbed his shoulder, kneading into the muscles. More hurt than he let on.

"I brought you here because I needed to touch ground." The admission was hard, but he deserved the truth. "I couldn't hold shape in your world anymore, but I couldn't lose you, either." It was the truth, but somehow, deep inside, it felt like a lie.

He cast a glance at what I knew to him were only figures of shadow in the darkness. "You'll waste if you don't return to your origin," he said, guessing accurately.

His accuracy startled me. It seemed almost as though he'd stored away some dropped thread from the fraying tapestry of information I'd given him and pulled it out now to remind me.

I nodded, though I doubt he could truly see it, almost ashamed of the truth. This place had borne me. My magic was sourced in it, and I was exiled from it.

Sevina expected me to suffer a long death of wasting instead of making it quick at the hands of the Morrakai. Such was her rage and disappointment.

His mouth twitched as his gaze ran over Askrid and the way she was smoothing down her braids. Her eyes never wandered from his face, and yet she somehow was able to project hatred toward me.

Without shifting the direction of his body, he angled his face to mine. "These females wanted you dead."

"Want," I said, sighing as I corrected him. "It's just a matter of time before they achieve it."

I kneaded my own shoulders. A moment came and went while we studied each other, assessing the hunch of exhaustion and pain in each other's backs. One warrior recognizing another.

A sizzle moved through the air between us, something I felt more like a ripple of energy. Something that cupped my heart and gave it a squeeze.

I almost gasped at the sensation, but his voice cut it short.

"Do you feel that?" he asked, and I swallowed hard at the tightness in his voice.

I wanted to nod, to concede that yes, I did feel it. But since I couldn't name it, I did nothing except stand there awkwardly running my hands over my body, surveying with tentative fingers the damage done by the Sisters.

No broken bones, but a lot of bruising. Had he not intervened, likely I would be dead. For a heartbeat, nothing moved but the rise and fall of our breath.

The silence felt too loud, carrying with it whispers of memory that reminded me of how we were built, and what I'd torn down.

Built of a single Sidhe's escape from Aiofe's dungeons, the Nocturnes had clawed their way into existence. This mother of the Nocturnes, this Madre, had stolen a hundred others from Kumara's clutches, all female energies, all of various natal and innate magics.

But cloaking the realm within the realm took power, and the only way to gain power was to join with new and varied magics. Birth magic, death magic, those things became part of the source.

Raids into the upper realms became necessary, exposing the Sidhe to weak or untappable powers, the exploitation and abuse of violent fae who tortured them for sport and lust.

Such was the lore. Such was our despair.

Until a union of violence birthed a female who offered hope of a new world.

A seer. A Sacred She. A higher fae who could see magical signatures across the realms, predict when certain bloodlines were at their peak. Find a way to change everything from the vulnerability of the Nocturnes, to the way to gain a powerful weave of magic that kept them safe in isolation.

Between her and the Madre, they birthed the Morrakai, using the best of warrior magics raided from realms far and wide. The Morrakai became the raiders, the protectors, the best of the best. They offered their bodies to the quickening, drawing forth better, stronger magics. The Weave grew stronger.

Our powers grew. The collective weave of magic built hope and strength. And when the Sacred She's powers withered, and she found her death, another rose from the same line, and another and another.

I had taken our generation's from the Nocturnes. Without Enyali, the prescience needed to find the best, the most powerful magics to match ours and intensify the source, was lost.

And they hated me for it.

I looked out over the square, and the hills beyond, took in the torches that lined the path to the temple, and the Morrakai as they glared at me and Stone, the ones who circled the Madre, and I knew a sort of shame.

I'd raided, and I'd killed, and as the only surviving Sidhe from the line of the Sacred She, I could have done more to protect the source.

I was still musing over the thought when the air crackled with a different sort of energy. Something had changed, the result, no doubt, of the Madre's conference with her guard.

I barely had time to register the change in the air, a charged ribbon of electricity.

One moment, it was just him and me—too close, too intense—and the next, the darkness screamed.

A dozen high-pitched and keening clicks cut through the air, loud enough, sharp enough that it even hurt my ears.

Most of it was coming from the Morrakai.

Stone went completely still.

But I sank to my haunches, unable to stand beneath the weight of what that sound meant for us both.

Chapter 9

IN AN EARLIER LIFETIME, I'd killed at the behest of the Madre without question or guilt. Now, the echoes of those murders whispered of blame coming home to roost. A dozen males went beneath my blade alone, season after season. So I knew well the sound of The Keening.

I knew what it meant when Sevina stepped forward and the Sisters circled her, each emitting her own pitch of echolocation, voices unique and familiar.

The noise grew to a crescendo, the ticks and snaps accelerating and growing louder until they drummed on tiny bones in my ears, making them ring and ache.

Stone didn't stop up his ears as he had earlier. He held his chin high, defiance carving his jawline into a hard cut of marble as he cast a challenge through his gaze and scanned the shadows and the figures that surrounded us.

"Has your vision adjusted?" I asked him, leaning closer so that my shoulder almost brushed his, trying not to give voice to the dread urgency climbing my spine at the sight of the Sisters moving into place around us. I counted fifty of them, and I felt a pang. Our numbers were dwindling. "Can you see better?"

"I can see shapes," he whispered back. I caught the warmth of his breath and heard in his voice an intimacy that suggested the companionship of warriors about to risk their lives together in battle.

But if he didn't understand exactly what was happening, he at least realized the danger, and I appreciated that.

"It may improve more," I said. "If you're here long enough for that to happen."

His eyes narrowed, and he shifted closer as well. "If? You make it sound as though I won't be." The wariness in his voice proved just how intuitive he could be.

My sisters murmured together. This close to Stone, I knew they could see him well enough. Not as clearly as I could, but they could tell what I had brought home. They were eager.

"Come with me," I said, pointing to the temple door and praying he would sense the movement and obey even if he couldn't see it. "Come now before it's too late."

He stiffened enough that I could see how tight his jawline was. Beyond him, the Sisters had begun to murmur, their voices low and throaty. I reached out my hand to his, a desperate gesture, and I felt the pulling of energy between us, sticky as cold molasses stringing out along fingertips.

I didn't really expect him to take my hand like some child looking for protection, but I did hope he'd at least pivot toward the temple door. The shape, the cut outline of the hammered copper, was obvious even in the darkness. Sanctuary. They wouldn't dare harm us there.

A murmur from my sisters caught his attention, though, and he peered back over his shoulder, wary as a hare being chased by a pack of wolves. "What are they saying?"

"They aren't speaking a foreign tongue,' I snapped, feeling the desperation of the moment, wanting him to understand I needed his trust. "You know exactly what they're saying."

"They're arguing." His voice was flat, as though he didn't want to believe the evidence of his own ears.

While I pitied him right then, I couldn't take the time to indulge it. Too much was at stake.

I took a step toward him. "Please," I said. "Just trust me. Just this once."

He was seething. Even I could see that, and I wasn't great at reading such clues.

But then, flames leapt down the pathway, jumping from torch to torch as someone, likely Sevina, used her magic to throw light on the entirety of the temple and square.

The sisters, the Morrakai, and even Sevina reared back from the sudden flare of light.

In the brilliance that peeled back the shadows, familiar faces and shapes revealed each secret wrinkle and formation. Some had high fae forms with arms and legs and delicate features. A few, those who were more base of the Shadow Sidhe, of older stock, were more creature than fae.

Of those, some possessed horns of varying shapes and sizes. Some owned wings that they folded over themselves like cloaks. A few grew lumps on their skin that resembled fungus on a dying tree. One resembled a walking serpent.

Not all were bipedal. All were female.

Stone was as used to seeing the myriad fae forms as I was. He didn't gasp at what met his gaze, though I knew he didn't expect such a motley clan.

But he took an involuntary step back toward me. I knew it wasn't because of the way they looked. It was the way they looked at *him*.

"Stone?"

This time, I couldn't disguise the note of panic. His head turned sharply toward my voice, and I knew he'd heard it too. The nod he gave me might have eased the tightness in my throat, but it was too late.

Sevina had already lifted a hand into the air above her head. She sliced down.

And silence fell.

My heart could have turned to ice in that moment. My whole body went clammy as she held her palm out straight. A brief but beautiful glow of silver light gathered on her palm. That tight, viselike grip fear had of my throat spread to my chest and bloomed to full panic at the sight of it.

"Fuck," I said and grabbed for Stone's arm.

We could run, I thought. I could head for the ley line Enyali had built and pull him back with me to the lands of daylight and reverse all this that I'd brought down on him. Give him his life back. Take my own.

The muscle in his biceps flexed and tightened beneath my fingers. Desperately, I willed my magic around me.

But the light in Sevina's palm had already solidified. My own magics paused, sniffing at the taste of power in the air like a mouse smelling fresh seed. I lost the feel of the ley lines as they dropped away from me. The exile, for the moment, was paused, and the source in the grounds, the air, the mist, all clarified.

It was like a moment of rapturous existence. The feeling of belonging, of knowing euphoria, of coming home, suffused me.

A sting of tears burned into my eyelids at the rush of euphoria. I could no more leave than I could stop breathing. Beneath my hand, his biceps flexed and let go, reminding me of his presence, that I wasn't alone. That I'd come here for a reason.

And yet, I arched backward, surrendering to the sensation of joining with the whole of the Nocturnes, pulling Stone with me as I strained to join the source, so much bigger than the tiny taste Enyalia had left me on the threshold of her sacred space.

Groundless, footless, I moved on the magic off the steps and along the torchlit path.

I was unaware of Stone's struggles. My magic had him in as tight a clasp as the Nocturnes had me. If he bit me, punched, kicked, or tried to strangle the air from my lungs, I felt nothing. Just the primal desire to be as I was born, that overcame every other thought.

Wings I'd not felt so much as twitch in a generation slid free of my body, brushing against his cheek and jaw as they unfurled. They spread with rapturous abandon on the air. Magic gathered in the spaces between each plume and feather, and I could imagine them for the first time in decades, glinting in the torchlight with the iridescence of abalone.

I almost sobbed in release. I savored it, letting it coat me like a warm slick of oil.

And it was in that instant of rapture and peace that I trapped us.

Whether I let go of Stone or he managed to wrest himself from me, I didn't know. But we both stood on packed earth instead of black flagstone, some-where between the temple steps and the square. Close enough to the Sisters that I could make out a dozen of them holding chunks of various sizes of ivory between their hands.

When Sevina stepped out of the boundary of bodies and into the space inside the circle they made around us, she held up her own glistening white hunk of bone.

She hefted it in a swing behind her, preparing to lob it at us. I felt Stone go rigid.

"She isn't going to stone you," I said in a tight voice, but stepped half in front of him anyway before I could stop myself.

The other sisters took a respectful step backward, giving Sevina space to cast her lot.

When it landed, it fell short of where we stood. A bleached-looking thing too stark against the darkness of earth. It wasn't large, but it drew every gaze for a long moment as everyone considered what it might mean for the aged Madre to cast for a male.

A knuckle bone. Smoothed between worrying fingers over generations to a round pebble that showed bubbles of petrified marrow.

I dropped my head back. "My fault," I whispered in a husky voice. "I'm so sorry, Stone. So damned sorry."

His name felt heavy on my tongue, like a guilty confession in a sacred space.

Because I knew what his fate would be then because of my weakness. I knew the inevitable consequence of bringing him, like I should have known it all along.

I clamped my lips together, dragging in a breath through my nose as the bone wobbled and fell to rest. For a moment, he stared down at the chunk of ivory dumbfounded.

The utter silence of the square was unnerving. The sisters had gone silent. The tension was so palpable, my heart felt like it was going to pound its way through my rib cage.

"The blade sings at her whisper," Sevina said in intonation, a prayer of rote making her voice raspy as paper being scorched by flame. "The Mother speaks through her tongue."

Stone glanced at me, and in the time it took to catch my eyes and open his mouth to speak the question I knew sat on his lips, the air began to rain with knuckles and heels and skulls as more sisters tossed in their lots.

"Too late," I said without meaning to speak. "It's way way way too late."

Stone swung in a circle at the sound of my voice, watching more lengths of bone fly in and land around his feet. They littered the ground around him. Shin bones, femurs. A piece of skull. Someone had tossed in a hunk of pitted pelvis, a macabre echo that also served to foreshadow the tosser's intent.

To me, it looked like every one of my sisters cast their lot for him, save the ones who were too young. A pang of guilt rose to my throat as I watched Stone struggling to hide his confusion behind a mask of stoic disinterest.

"What in the holy gods is going on?" he demanded.

My eyes closed on their own, refusing to take in one more inch of the scene.

"Life," I said. "And death. That's what's going on."

"What have you done?" he asked me in a soft exhale that came like a gentle breeze over my skin.

The warm, cocooning scent of caramel and butter moved over the air. No accusation, though it should have been. Only the ache of bewilderment and that nearly undid me more than any righteous anger could.

"I lost you," I said, voice cracking.

My head hung, and I squeezed my eyes closed. I didn't want to look at the assemblage of bones lying scattered around his feet.

I stooped, thinking to pluck one of the lots from the ground, but even as I considered it, a ruckus sounded in the circle. The volume of clicks and clacks grew loud enough to draw my eyes to where another sister had stepped outside the formation and into the ring beside Sevina.

Askrid didn't need the distance cut short to cast her lot perfectly. She was strong and efficient in every movement she made. What she'd done, stepping inside the circle, standing next to the Madre was done for drama.

The Morrakai leader paused for effect, shooting me a long look before she tossed her bone in a perfect arc, proving the aim was a practiced one.

It landed atop the instep of Stone's left boot.

"No raid rides blind," she said, lifting her chin at me. "The seer draws the map in blood and bone and the sisters accept the sacrifice."

The words drew my gaze to her face. Enyali's words. Chosen at this moment by the leader of the raiding parties, both a warning and a threat for me.

Askrid. She who'd borne five sisters for the Nocturnes during her breeding lifetime, the highest number any one sister had gifted. Her offspring were strong and resilient. Their magics were varied and powerful. With shoulders as broad as her hips, the very squareness of her physique made her a solid warrior.

That aim hadn't just been practiced by casting for males over the generations. She was the Nocturne's fiercest fighter, leading dozens of raids in her time.

She was the one who trained me in the ways of the Morrakai. A mentor who both groomed me for battle as determinedly as she groomed me to be her lover. A female I'd raided beside and whose advances I'd rejected.

She'd hated me ever since.

"I cast for him," she said. Not a shout. That wasn't her style. But it was projected loudly. Proudly.

"You're too old," another Sister muttered beneath her breath, but it drew sudden, electric silence from the circle.

Askrid didn't turn around to confront the sister who'd spoken in bitter rebuke. She merely pinned her gaze to Stone's shoulders and said without malice or emotion to no one in particular, "Test me in the challenge, then, and see how old I am."

No one cast again after that, and I had the feeling she'd waited until every sister who wanted Stone, had made their bid to win him before she'd tossed her own lot.

Seeing this, Sevina held out her hand toward the litter of ivory pieces all but glowing white against the black earth. Her piece of knuckle bone lifted from the ground and sailed into her grip. She curled her fingers around it.

"Those who wish to, may retract their lots," she said to the formation of Morrakai.

Few sisters had the magic of transmutation the way Sevina did. To reclaim their lots, the sisters would have to get close enough to Stone to pick them up.

No one did. Stone swung his gaze to mine. When he stepped toward me, his boots crunched on fragments of bone. "What in the heck is going on?"

I was careful to keep on his nondominant side. "You heard them arguing before," I said. "You know what they were arguing about."

He looked unsettled. "They were arguing about how many would get a chance to try me." He swallowed. "They mean to fight me. Perhaps to the death? Perhaps to steal my magic?"

My lips pressed tight together. Not knowing how the Nocturnes worked, of course he would think he was going to die here. And he wasn't wrong.

"You're not entirely wrong," I said. "They will fight, but it will be sister against sister, and not against you. They will take each other on, hand to hand, and the winner will have you as her prize."

The words tasted bitter. I reached for the weapon on my back automatically, the one that I'd left behind in his world, in the room that was his, where his scent lingered on the sheets I'd woken to.

And when I realized what I was doing, my hands fell to my sides, shoulders sagging. I'd brought him here. I'd taken on the job. The inevitable could only benefit me. And yet when I said the words, they felt hollow.

"And *then* you will die."

Chapter 10

THE FIRST MALE I'D slain had left puberty behind by mere days. I'd taken him during my first raid to the realm of daylight from a small village, where he was practicing his magic in moving things with his mind. He wasn't a shimmering high fae; rather, he was a plain sort of thing that might have human blood in his veins. But he showed promise in the size and heft of things he could control, and so I took him from the fragrant garden where his family lived in a small roundhouse with chalk-lined walls and an herb garden bordering the pigpen.

Enyali had foreseen this raid, saying it wasn't in his mere ability in telekinesis to our weave, but in the things his seed might bring later.

The boy served well in The Quickening. I could still hear the ruckus of victory as, one by one, the sisters took him to their chambers. Still smelled the smoke and aroma of roasting meat as he gave his last offering to the Nocturnes.

But then the smell of roasted flesh dissolved. The square slammed back into focus.

Sevina was moving again—headed straight for the temple steps. As she passed by me, I thought of that piece of ivory and imagined her robbing it from its cradle of velvet and alabaster, and I froze. Any thought of striking out at her, of catching her back to prevent her from entering was robbed from me.

Stone had no such reservations.

He launched himself at the Madre in a move so silent and swift, even the Morrakai of her personal guard were surprised into inaction for a solid moment.

He managed to hook her by the throat for several heart-stopping seconds. Her power plumed above her, released like a spectral mist, and for an instant I thought he might have killed her and released her magics to the realm.

I was paralyzed by the possibility as he swung her around to face the sisters, legs dangling, head angled frighteningly forward. A moment might pass, but no more before the Morrakai rushed to her rescue, and throttled him into mere tissue and blood regardless of his potential to seed new magic.

That rampage was all I could think of, and my legs moved before my brain engaged, that long ingrained instinct to fight coming to my aid.

Elbow snapping out, I took down the first of the guards who tried to reach him. My wings flapped out and came down in an extension of my arms, pinning her to the earth while I kicked at her ribs. A smile seamed my lips at the satisfying sound of bone cracking.

No magic. Not against each other. We wouldn't waste any source that we didn't need to.

I found as I brought my bare foot down once more that I didn't need it.

But then, the guards swarmed Stone, and Sevina disappeared beneath the fray.

Askrid yanked me away, tossing me to the steps like a rag, and I fell on my ribs.

By the time I propped myself up again, Stone was standing off to the side, chest heaving, lips curled back. His black hair bristled. He wore the aura of a panther outlining his fae self, and though he seemed very much more like a vicious dog, I had the sense that he might be able to shift if he wanted. Transformation magic. Not something the Nocturnes had seen in a while.

He was magnificent. And frightening. Even the Morrakai eyed him with awed respect and stood back, fists curling and uncurling against their sides. Askrid glowered at him through a black eye.

But Sevina, who stood beside the temple door, her palm pressed against the hammered surface, merely looked back over her shoulder, unimpressed and unfazed by his attack.

"Enough," she said. Her voice was thready with age, but there was still that same powerful note of command in it.

I shot Stone a look of pity that he returned with rage. My heart squeezed. Strong as he was, a lone fae male couldn't compete with a dozen Nocturne warriors. But there wasn't time to worry about his ego. The Madre was about to enter the temple.

Struggling to my feet, I gathered my power, and I lifted my chin.

"Sevina," I called out. "Face me. Acknowledge me. Do not enter my sister's space without taking me with you."

The Madre back-stepped three paces to meet me where I stood. Her fingers crooked beneath my chin, forcing my eyes upward onto hers.

She looked like a breath could evaporate her into smoke. But I wasn't fooled. I knew her power, the command she held over the entire Morrakai.

Her clouded eyes scoured my face. "It is a great gift you offer the Nocturnes," she said.

My mouth barely moved for the anger. "I didn't come bearing gifts."

The smile that spread over her face might have warmed any of the other sisters' hearts. It sent a chill down mine. "No. You came trying to steal what no longer is yours to claim." She flicked her wrist, and Askrid's hand shot out with whipping speed to hook my elbow.

I tried to wrench free, glaring from one to the other. "He was not raided," I snapped. "You have no right to him. He's mine. I took him from his world."

"And we took him from you," Sevina said. "He now belongs to the Casting."

Stone roared his protest but was swiftly shut down by a cloud of black mist. Sevina. Showing her power.

"You can't do that." I pulled at Askrid's hold, and she slammed me against the temple wall. My breath leaked free with the force of impact.

"You forget yourself, Morvannon," she said. "You have no voice here."

Wheezing, I glared at her, lip curled. "You wanted my voice once," I hissed. "Wanted it to beg you, to shower you with words of desire."

"That was decades ago when you showed promise." She bared her teeth at me as she looked down at me.

"None of that matters," Sevina said, pulling Askrid's attention away from my face. "The sisters have made their intentions known. He has been cast for. It is done. Bring him inside." She shot a cutting glance my way. "And remove the Morvannon."

Askrid swept me off the temple steps. I fought, kicking and writhing as they dragged him away from me, shoving him toward the door.

"Wait," I yelled, finding a gap in Askrid's defenses to elbow her in the nose. Though she teared up, she did not release me.

By then, Stone was fighting back hard. Each inch the warriors succeeding in moving him was hard won. It took one of them to punch him in the throat to control him, and that only for a moment.

Sevina watched it all with interest, her head canted to the side thoughtfully. "He is a strong one," she said and gestured at Askrid to release me. Stone's captors fell back as well, and he stumbled from the sudden release.

"What of his magic, Morvannon?" she demanded. "He has yet to use a single ounce of power. What possessed you to bring him with you when you touched ground?"

It was an opening. One I could use if I was cunning enough. She was beginning to doubt he was worthwhile. That the sisters might waste themselves on him.

I jerked my chin toward the temple. "Inside," I said, sensing that if I could get her away from the rest of the Sisters, I might be able to persuade her to abandon the casting. "You and I. I'll explain everything."

She ran her palm down the hammered copper, her fingers playing over the runes. "I've not been inside since she died," she said, and her voice carried a surprising grief. That buoyed me enough to press her.

"It's because of her I come," I said.

That got her attention. She couldn't push open the door fast enough, and as I followed her in, found my gaze searching for Stone.

"Leave him," she said as though she felt my eyes meeting his and directing him to follow. "The only business he has in this sacred space has not yet begun."

"About that…" I began but lost track of the thought as the sight of the interior left me gasping as I crossed the threshold.

The sacred temple, the place where Enyali spent so much of her time, had fallen not just into disrepair, but into dereliction.

The black marble floors, shot through with silver veins, sat beneath a layer of dust so thick it made a noise when I walked through it. The scent of old magic clung to the stones like a memory, her fragrance, a hint of rosemary and ozone.

The space felt smaller than I remembered—stripped, hollow, starved of magic.

I brushed a hand along the wall, fingers leaving trails in dust, and catching on cobwebs that clung from ceiling to wall, sticky enough to knot into a ball as I moved through.

I doubted Sevina could see the interior as well as I could, and yet she found the stone bench without trouble. She brushed at the surface, shoveling dirt away from it like snow.

"She would be heart broken," I said, watching the wrinkled sheet of filth shed the bench.

Sevina lowered herself onto the only stone bench in the navel of the temple and crossed one ankle over the other. Here, her skin looked less like parchment and more like the high fae she'd been born of, with that soft sheen glowing beneath the surface. It made me think that maybe some of Enyali's magic was left in the temple after all.

The bench was for the supplicants, the ones who wanted their fortunes scried, or those of the warrior caste who needed inspiration for the raids.

I'd sat there many times, silent and patient, waiting for Enyali to complete her rituals for the month, adding my energy to hers so she could hasten back to the role of being just a sister.

My own gaze followed Sevina's to the pedestal in the heart of the sanctuary. But while Sevina would see only an empty chair and dried-up basin, I imagined my sister there again, bathed in the sacred light of the crystals above us. My entire body felt weighted down with lead.

The vision was so powerful, I startled when Sevina's voice broke the silence.

"We have left it untouched out of reverence," she said. "We have held only one Quickening here since she went to Kumara."

I stole another glance at the Madre, considering her sickly pallor, the tissue-thin skin. I knew well enough how the Quickening worked. It took a lot of power, and she no doubt suffered to bring life into the wombs of the sisters, ensuring the seeds of the sires took root.

That didn't excuse her leaving Enyali's place filthy and untended. Anger burned in my chest, and when I spoke, it leaked into my voice like an errant tongue of flame.

"How is it reverent to leave her place abandoned of all care?" I gestured at the altar. For a moment, I imagined my sister there, and my heart choked out an anemic heartbeat.

If Sevina heard the emotion in my voice, she ignored it, instead choosing to smooth down her hair and brush out the wrinkles in her linen tunic.

"I will have it cleaned and prepared," she said, her gaze also going to the altar. "This ceremony is special, and the temple should reflect that." Legs uncurling, she placed her hands on her thighs as though she'd made a momentous decision and was done with me. "He's magnificent," she said. "The sisters all want him. You have done well."

I cast an eye toward a cranny carved into the altar where an alabaster box gathered cobwebs and dust. My eyes squeezed closed at the sight of it, memories of the youth who had given himself willingly on that raid so long ago. He was a fae of adventure, I thought, bored with his banal life. His excitement at the thought of travel, of discovering his part in the Casting of Bones meant he would bed several beautiful Sidhe the likes of which would be far above his reach in his world.

He seeded a single Morrakai that season. Despite being young, and despite the Madre's decision to forgo the traditions of the challenge, he was passed about to any Morrakia female who wished it.

I was expected to participate. But Enyali insisted it wasn't my time to bear children for the Nocturnes.

So when he was done with his duties to my sisters, and one warrior knew she was carrying another generation, my blade slid across his throat.

I consumed him piece by piece, both raw and roasted. I drank his blood and saved part of his body as a casting trophy.

That bone remained unused for years through Enyali's predictions that it was to be left virgin until my fated mate came to the Nocturnes. That, to do anything else would rob the Sisters of the greatest warrior they'd ever produce.

It languished in that box untouched for all these years. A delicate wrist bone that I imagined was still yellow and rough. I trembled at the thought of it.

"Stone is not a peace prize," I said. "I brought him here because I spent too long tracking him. I wasn't about to lose his trail just to touch the source again."

Sevina's eyes narrowed, and a hateful gleam flared beneath the shuttered lids. "He is one of your fares, then," she intoned in a tight voice.

"Yes."

The way she looked at me, silent, and thoughtful, I thought she could see through to my scrambling thoughts. I'd never truly known how much power Sevina possessed. No one spoke of the limits of her magic or the nature of it. But she always seemed to know the heart of a sister.

She stood and brushed off her tunic. "Then whoever paid for his death won't mind him being put to service first so long as he dies."

"I will mind."

She canted her head at me. "You will mind? I thought the Morvannon incapable of minding anything but the coin she earns from selling magics that belong here. To your sisters."

I lifted my chin. "My magics are my own."

"As are mine, and yet I share them with the realm because that's what it means to be of the Nocturnes."

She spread her arms wide, the linen shift hiking up around her shoulders and showing thin cords and thin skin. "I could keep my magic to myself but I give it freely. So the sisters may live without giving themselves to Kumara."

"Some life," I spat out. "Neither living nor dead. Not true fae but not thralls of the queen either." My chest began to ache. "This place is one of wasting."

"So speaks one who straddles realms with the ease of breath," she said, bitterness swelling in her tone.

In all my years, I'd never seen Sevina leave the Nocturnes. I'd always presumed it was because she preferred the darkness the same as the others. That their eyes, so accustomed to pitch, would truly go blind in the daylight.

"You can't have him," I said.

She sighed through her nose. "But we have taken him," she said. "And he is marked for death anyway so this short sojourn here will not matter in the end."

"Aiofe purchased that death," I blurted out. "The Queen of the Stygian Darkness made the blood vow with me to extinguish his life."

I could swear Sevina paled all the way to her bare feet at the words. She certainly went silent. So silent that I found it difficult to stand still. A glance at Enyali's perch drew my feet as surely as my gaze. I found myself standing beside it, my palm flattening against the surface. I conjured her face to my mind's eye because I didn't want to think about the shape of shadow that made up her energies there in Kumara.

"I saw her there," I said, musing aloud, maybe for my benefit more than Sevina's. "Enyali, I mean. She is wasted and enthralled to the queen."

My mind roamed to the restlessness of Kumara, the sensation of being pulled to the queen no matter how badly I wanted to leave. I knew Enyali's restless energy as she struggled to maintain what magics she'd earned in the darkness. I knew she hoped to come home again.

She stood suddenly, her linens hanging from her body in long folds. Stretching back, she planted her hands on her hips as though to free her spine from a crick in the shape. "Enyali belongs to the Nocturnes," she said. "She should be here, favoring us with her magics. But for you, we would still have her."

My head snapped up at her approach. "You think I don't know that?" I demanded. "Why do you think I made the blood vow with Aiofe? Why do you think I couldn't lose track of him, why I brought him here with me when I felt the pull of the Nocturnes demanding I touch ground."

If I expected understanding, I was naïve. Instead of seeing the possibilities of Stone's death bringing Enyali life, Sevina scalded me with a look that dropped me to my knees on the temple floor. I felt a suffusing blast of power. The scent of ozone and old blood crested over me and clouded around me. My body felt as if it was going to implode from the rise of her magics.

Cheek pressed against the cool black marble, hands beside my head, I braced for her power to overcome me and prayed it would not. Not because I was afraid of death or pain, but because I knew I was Stone's best chance of survival. If I didn't hold the line now, he would die here.

Instead of bearing down on me with her power, Sevina lifted her voice in a banshee wail that cut through my ears like a shard of glass. Even used to the echolocation noises of the sisters, I feared my hearing would be damaged from her anger alone.

"You bargained with the Queen of the Stygian Darkness?" she said in a scathing tone when she expended her breath. "Fool."

She took to pacing the temple from navel to head and back again, feet slapping on the marble noisily. "You realize the threat you have brought down upon us." The face that had paled earlier grew red as a daylighter sunrise. "If she senses him here, if she knows you broke your vow, she will scour our Nocturnes and strip the flesh from our bones to boil in her river."

My head hung. I knew it was true. I also knew Sevina would not let this chance to use new power slip through her fingers.

"I did not break my vow," I said, daring to lift my face from the earth and pin my gaze to her feet. Her toes were webbed together, bony and thin. I swallowed, waiting to see if she'd strike me down with her magic. "I kept it."

When she did nothing but breathe above me, I raised my gaze to her knees, to her hands at her sides. To her face, finally. There was interest in her expression. A good sign, I hoped.

"If you haven't broken your vow, then we still have time," she said. "We'll take our chances for one long-night."

A flare in my chest, like a bolt of lightning. A long-night. In daylighter terms, that meant twenty four hours. I could regain a lot of source in that time. I carefully smothered the feeling of hope.

"Thank you, Madre," I said, bowing once more to brush a breath against her toes, the best sign of respect I could offer without touching lips to skin. "We will take our leave after the long-night. All I ask is that we are allowed to seek rest here in this sacred space."

I didn't want to say I didn't trust the sisters to leave us alone. That they wouldn't dare defile the temple. But I also didn't want to take the chance that outside this sanctuary, I might be vulnerable to a queen come looking for her due and finding herself cheated.

The Madre had other thoughts, it seemed.

"We?" she asked with a sniff. "You may leave, Morvannon, as you wish, but the male remains."

Panic clamped like a vise over my voice box. I struggled to protest and only sputtered out words that had no meaning. "But I thought—"

"You misunderstand then. The sisters have cast for him. It is done. He will spend this long night with all who have bid for him, and then he will die by the rites of the Hollowing and his wasted magic can return to Aiofe as your vow decreed. Your vow will be honored and you will have earned your long-night's worth of magic. Enough to keep you from having to touch down for more than a decade."

She picked up a small crystal from the altar, a leftover from Enyali's scrying bowl, and examined it.

"Any other fae would call that victory. Take it, Ruby. It is all the gift you will receive here."

Chapter 11

SEVINA SWEPT MY HANDS from her legs and turned to the temple door. In moments she would be gone, and with her my hopes of getting Enyali back.

But there was something more, something disturbing that didn't occur to me until I felt the blood drain from my face at the memory of how Stone's skin felt giving way beneath my blade. The sensation of the vow settling in. Knowing I'd completed my fare.

And the strange sensation of elation I'd felt later when I realized that despite my completion of my vow, he was somehow still alive.

"Please," I murmured, desperate for some reason. I scrambled to my feet, thinking to follow her.

She swiped across her throat with her thumb. "It's done," she said. "I will send sisters in to sanctify the space anew. And then we will deliver your male to the first sister."

She cracked open the door to the temple, and torch-light flooded in, making a neat triangle on the black marble. When she stepped into the glow, I saw just how thin she'd grown.

"Sevina," I said, trying my best sense of urgency, but she was already striding out into the square, leaving me behind.

I caught sight of Stone sitting with his legs crossed, bruised, swollen, and smirking.

"He already died," I shouted at her retreating back. "I killed him already but he didn't die."

That stopped her in her tracks.

"Explain," she said.

"Aiofe wants him," I said. "That means she wants his powers. Whatever his natal and innate magics are, she was willing to have him killed to acquire them."

Sevina stooped, though gods knew how she balanced on the thin reeds of her legs. Eye to eye, she searched my face.

"You brought him here because you knew we would want him as well," she said.

I didn't agree, but I didn't argue either. "I brought him here because I want to barter him for Enyali's life, and he is safe nowhere else until she is home again and gazing into her basin."

"It has been ages since the sisters have had an oracle," she mused aloud. "Too many decades, so many I've lost count."

"Six and a half. Three Annums. Five days." I said, correcting her.

She gave me a look that pulled more words from my chest than I would have wanted her to hear from me. They came out on a bitter tide that stung my lips. "You think it strange that I have counted the passing of seasons without my sister? The years I have been banished from my home?"

So many emotions I had buried and forgotten, but I recognized the look of sympathy on her face. I knew the feeling of pity when her fingers brushed my cheek. Knew them both and hated her for it even as I bore her touch because I needed to.

"Enyali had a great gift," she said. "I'm surprised you owned none of her power being blood-borne. Had you just once cast for a male, just once lain with one long enough to beget a daughter, perhaps we wouldn't be without an oracle. You are from the line. The only line. You had a duty—"

I held up my hand. "I wanted Enyali back," I said. "*She* is the oracle. *She* is the seer. Not some spectre of a fae child no one could even predict would be a female, let alone one with the sight gift."

"And she is wasted," Sevina spat out. "Because of you."

Another judgment. As though I hadn't hated myself for it all this time. I let the accusation slide because it was a moot point. Even if I had the power of a seer's magic the way Enyali did, I would not have used it. To do so was to surrender the hope that the sisters would fight the queen to retrieve her.

"The queen hired you to kill him?"

I knew she understood that the queen of the Stygian Darkness wanted him dead so she could claim his power. So, I nodded, the only answer I could give in light of the confusion I still felt at the thought that the queen of all the underworld fae realms needed something from a daylighter fae.

Sevina seemed to accept that simple response. As though her arms weren't brittle as sticks that threatened to break in an errant breeze, she reached down and hooked my shoulder, using her leverage to lift me to my feet as she straightened up. It was an effortless movement for her, the grip on my armpit strong and unyielding.

The old madre had strength left, it seemed. I wasn't sure why I was surprised.

"The sisters will harbor your prize," she said to me, looking back at the door of the temple as though she could see through the hammered copper to the square beyond. "And they will make use of him while he's available."

I understood that the moment they had cast their lots for him in the square. I had hoped for it the moment I realized in the tavern that he might be of better service to me alive than dead.

"You will barter his life for Enyali's."

I nodded. "The queen herself offered me the same when she summoned me."

Sevina put a finger to her forehead, thinking, perhaps trying to wrest an iota of prescience from a dehydrated third eye. "If she already bartered for him, then why bring him here? Why not just deliver him to the queen and bring Enyali home? Why is she not already sitting on her pedestal, scrying our future and finding our far-flung seeds?"

There it was again. A flare of emotions that would have bowed me a lifetime ago, all traversing her face and posture. At one time, I would have named each emotion and felt it burn inside me. This time, like almost every time since Enyali's death, my heart flitted past them like a hummingbird ignoring poison ivy.

I sorted through my own feelings of guilt and shame and forced a slow walk through the memories and events that brought me here. I mind-jumped to Aiofe's throne room and sensed Enyali there, bleeding out magic she'd earned over a century. I skimmed through images of Stone with the women, the way he looked at me at the tavern when he realized I was from the darkness.

The hesitation I'd felt when I'd shot the blade from Irina's hand. The peculiar desire to touch his skin. The way his throat yielded to my blade and the gut punch that had stricken me moments before his fae horse had tried to kill me.

I could come up with only one answer that made sense.

"I vowed to kill him," I said, remembering the way my blade felt as I'd drawn it across his throat in the stables "And I did so."

I shifted my weight from one foot to the other as I reached out for the blood vow that bound me to the barter. Nothing flared back at me. No burn seared my soul. No itch bade me with adrenaline-soaked need to act.

There was only a blank canvas where that blood-infused etching should be.

My hands curled at my sides at the thought that I was free. "Stone survived my attack. But he should have died. My part in the bargain is over. The blood vow is unseated."

I followed her out into the square, where Stone stood, surrounded by the Morrakai.

"The vow is no more," I said, hurrying to catch up to her even as I wondered how a fae of her age could move so fast. "We don't have Aiofe's blessing to return Enyali. If he dies now we may never get her back."

Several sisters shifted their feet, confused. Stone's gaze found me, and his expression grew hard as though he had heard every word we'd spoken in the temple.

Sevina, however, didn't pause. Her treads were as focused and swift as they'd been when she'd left me behind.

"Madre," I called out. "You can't do this to us. To her."

She paused then, to stoop and pluck a ghost pipe orchid from its cluster. She twirled it in her fingers before turning to me. I waited, breath held, for her to answer.

When she did, her expression was stoic. "I may do what I think best for this realm. When you are Madre, you may dictate the terms of our rites. Until then, all I hear is that we have less time than we thought," she said. "That just means we must not delay."

"Like Hell," Stone yelled out, and one of the sisters clamped her hand over his mouth, whereupon he proceeded to thrash like a gator in the daylight world. His struggles did something to me, pulling me closer the way a cobra charms a mouse.

He was all but buried beneath a fray of sisters, struggling to fight back against their insistent pull.

"Leave him alone," I said, facing the sister who was putting her back into holding him still. She barely glanced at me.

"I said, leave him." I didn't wait for her to release him. My hand struck out before I even finished the command, knocking her aside.

Stone fell backward, and I shoved my way into the fray of sisters who had been tasked with keeping him silent and compliant. I leaned over him, reaching for his hand.

"Are you alright?" I asked, although he clearly was not. The bruises under his eyes had begun to seep.

He glared at me and slapped it away. "I don't need you," he said in a tight voice. That moment of peculiar camaraderie from before, of kindness in his eyes long gone.

I watched him get to his feet without using his hands. No magic. Just brute strength and flexibility. I couldn't tear my eyes from the pulse that throbbed in his neck, the way his shoulder muscles coiled and tensed and let go. I thought of a world robbed of him, and I couldn't breathe.

The Madre came up behind me. I felt her there, caught a whiff of that unique fragrance of earthen herbs and ozone.

"He won't suffer," she whispered. "Your sisters have taken male lovers before and know how to please them. They will give him a good death when they are done."

I spun on her. "Raped and tortured and slain like a beast in the dark wood."

She shrugged. "It has always been this way. You slayed a good many males in service to the Nocturnes." She eyed me with something I took as malice. "The only service you have given us."

A laugh bubbled free, and I shook my head. "You don't understand the magnitude of this," I said. "The vow is *gone*. The queen of the Stygian Darkness can't be trusted now that the vow is ended. He may die beneath our hands, but Enyali will remain in her wasteland, enthralled until she either dies the true death or finally regains enough magic to escape."

Poison laced my next words as I leveled my gaze at Sevina's throat. "Do you think she'll return here then? Knowing you gave up on her so you could take this male?" I snorted. "Even if she regains her magic in a thousand years, she'll never forgive you."

All the Madre did was cant her head at me, twirling the ghost pipe again. When she spoke, it was in a whisper. "Is it your sister's life you worry for now, Morvannon?" She inched closer. I could smell the woodsmoke on her linen. "It seems it's his fate that matters to you most."

My chest hurt. It wasn't rising and falling at all beneath my breath. She was wrong. Surely she knew the loneliness that made my marrow ache, the sensation of losing a limb, of a tooth that suddenly began to ache for no reason.

But then I thought of Stone with all the sisters, being forced to copulate, drugged with that damned ghost pipe that would make him weak and compliant, and then I imagined him going beneath the blade or the flames, and everything in my body hurt.

And I knew in that instant, the horror of the truth.

Stone, the male I'd tried to kill, the male who hated me, was my mate.

Chapter 12

I'D BEEN ALONE SO long I hadn't even considered that I might someday discover a connection strong enough to test the very fabric of my being. I'd always assumed Enyali to be the other half of me, the piece of my spirit that existed outside my body. Now, her words came back to haunt me. "He'll know you."

The realization that she'd known this all those decades ago when she'd insisted I hold back that piece of bone from that eager youth, took the air out of my lungs, the strength out of my knees.

But looking at Stone, feeling that sense of something snapping into place, I knew she'd been right. He hated me. Rightly so. I doubted he'd sensed the bond under this sort of duress if I'd only just realized it. The Nocturnes had a way of blanketing things in darkness that had nothing to do with a lack of light. Being new to it, his senses, his magics, and his energies were likely already overwhelmed.

Yet every instinct in me strained toward him, a draw I could not smother, no matter how I tried. And whether he knew or not, I couldn't let another sister, let alone dozens of them, have the right to his body.

"They have cast for you," I said to Stone. "Do you know what that is? Do you understand what they mean to do?"

His gaze traveled the faces of the surrounding warriors before dragging over Sevina, and finally cutting toward me.

"They seek to court me," he said, a delicate but sarcastic euphemism weighing down his voice with contempt.

"They seek to drug you," I explained, advancing on him. "They will use the ghost pipe in a drink to lower your resistance, and The Madre will cast the magic that will bring on their ovulation so that you may seed their wombs with daughters."

He looked at me with a quiet, cold assessment—as if calculating whether I was warning him for his sake or simply describing the process before taking my turn at him. The distrust was so sharp it stung my skin.

When he spat on the ground, I heard the force it took. His jaw went tight as his lips curled back. "Let them try."

He glared at each one and I inched close enough to him I could touch him if I wanted. My hand lifted and hovered in the air. He traced the path of my fingers, a softness gathering in his face.

A spark of energy jumped between us, prickling, tingling, and I wondered if he felt it too, but then he hardened his gaze, dropping my arm like a lead weight beside my thigh.

When his scent reached me, the distinct aroma of cinnamon and adrenaline, my pulse stuttered.

"You may fight," I said, worry coating my voice. "You may well take a few sisters out of commission, maybe give a few the true death, but you will succumb. We have done this thing for hundreds of years. We know how to make the most powerful fae bend to our will."

"I'll kill any who touch me." His shoulders squared as he gave me a pointed look. "Any."

The Madre laughed, and Askrid brandished the bone she'd cast earlier. "What is this nonsense," she demanded of Sevina. "Why are you entertaining this ludicrous discourse. Let us begin the challenges. Time is wasting."

A roar of agreement went up from the Marrakai and all those who hadn't cast but stood back, watching the proceedings with a bloodlust that sent the clicks and clacks into a cacophony that pitched into notes so high they made the temple door rattle.

Sevina held up her hand, silencing them.

"There will be no challenges," she said, and though the words renewed the uproar of clicks and snaps and sharp-toned noises, Stone didn't so much as cover his ears. I knew the sound was likely splitting his skull. I was sure I felt it in the air between us. I also felt his iron will. He wouldn't show weakness. Not for them. Not for anything.

Sevina seemed to revel in the anger, letting it grow to a pitch that carried with it a smothering weight of energy. I guessed it was to make her seem like a magnanimous monarch when she delivered the truth she'd already told me inside the temple.

"Hold, sisters," she intoned, loud and clear, her voice ringing in the air. Little by little, the sounds dissipated into blackened silence. "Each of us who cast earlier may have access to this specimen. No need to fight one another for the right to claim his magics. All may add his weave to theirs."

The words brought a collective gasp to the realm, my own the loudest in my ears. Stone, however, didn't show an iota of alarm in his posture.

"Just how fucking potent do you think I am?" Stone mumbled in a bitter voice. He jerked his head toward the pile of bones cast now in a pile. "Even a god couldn't rise to such service let alone in service to such nasty looking bitches."

He grinned, then, delighting in the rage that crossed Sevina's face. Shaking his head, he straightened his shoulders, emboldened, it seemed, by his own bravado.

"Mind you," he growled. "I might be persuaded to make a few of you choke on the cock you want so much, not out of pleasure, but to force the last breath out your asses."

His voice shook at the edges like paper being frayed. It was a note of silent admission, not fear but rage at his helplessness. As if to disguise it, he laughed, dropping his head back and letting the sound bellow out of his lungs. I thought he might have gone mad in the moment until he leveled his gaze on me.

"You knew you were bringing me to this," he ground out. "You will be the first to die."

My feet shuffled side to side as my head hung. I expected his ire. I deserved it. But he didn't know. He couldn't know. He'd been in the daylight world, where he could choose his lovers, where he could enjoy a female's touch.

That would not happen here. They would not serve him pleasure this night. Not now. Not ever.

They were awed by his strength. They respected it. But that just made them more determined to make him pay for it. They would rule him and use him, and then when all was done, they would slay him because in the Nocturnes, only the females lived with hope of a future.

Sevina's grin was wicked. "Have no fear, male of the damned. My magics are sufficient to bring you to rise over and over again all the way through the long-night." She chuckled as though she shared some intimate joke, and when the rest of the Morrakai did as well, I suspected she had.

He bared his teeth. "Then I will cut it off," he ground out. "I will sever it from my body before I choke each one of you with it."

A murmur went up through the Morrakai, one of anticipation of a good and violent promise. My stomach hollowed out. Even if he fought back, he couldn't win. I'd seen this play out too many times to hope for a good outcome.

The thought of him falling beneath their intentions, of those powerful shoulders sagging with impotence, his eyes growing dim from drugged compliance...I couldn't bear a moment more.

I turned and fled. My heart racing. His rejection still worming into my stomach and hollowing out a black place there, I aimed my feet for the temple steps.

He could hate me forever. I could take that. But this horror would not continue. I didn't care what it cost me.

With the laughter of my sisters at my back, and Stone's growling and cursing echoing behind me, I ran to the one place I knew held peace and sanity. My sanctuary. The one place in all my life that I felt safe.

Sevina's voice was already cutting through the din, intoning her magics to rise, drawing the power to the circle. I could almost smell the pheromones beginning to drift on the cool air.

Inside, I headed for the cranny where my own casting bone nestled inside that alabaster box. Even as my gaze fell on it my wings spread wide with a snap that startled me. I flew straight to it, dipping my hands into the well of the box and scooping it out into cradled hands.

And then I sailed back through the temple and out the door. In the middle of the square, Stone was clashing with Askrid, holding her at bay despite her many thrusts of spear and dancing steps of aggressive battle.

A heady perfume wafted through the air currents. Sevina looked plumper, rosier in the torchlight. Her hair had grown lush and painted in pink hues that caught the torchlight and swirled on touchless air currents.

I realized she hadn't been using her power all these years to drench the Nocturnes. She'd abandoned it to the realm, letting it have the best of her, and now she was pulling it back.

My wings folded over my back as I swooped over the center of the circle. I dropped with a thud to the ground, my feet feeling the energy of the source through my bare feet, lending me courage.

Spinning to face Sevina, I raised my knob of wrist bone, that boy flitting through my mind's eye as I did so.

It caught Sevina's attention. Her mouth formed a perfect O.

"I cast for this male," I bellowed. "I challenge any sister who thinks to take him as her own. I will tear her limbs from her body. I will devour her skin. I will swallow her blood in long slow drafts. Hear me. I swear it by the gods of the light and dark. Test me in this and find yourself at risk of true death."

Even as the words fled my lungs, the only thing I heard echoing inside me was a single undeniable, unbidden word.

Mine.

Chapter 13

THE BONE, WHEN I cast it, landed directly between Stone's feet. He looked down at it for a long moment before he lifted his gaze to mine and locked in.

For a second, there was no one else in the circle. A tendril of energy leaked out from my core, tentative, like a whisper of residual scent from a delicious meal. Every muscle in my body tensed and tightened.

"I cast for you, Stone of Terran," I whispered. "Though you loathe me, I do this to rectify the mistake I made in bringing you here, of accepting the queen's contract."

I thought he would reply. The words crossed his expression, and I almost could read them. But then Askrid charged the circle, spinning to face me.

And I knew the moment was over. He merely blinked at the chunk of bone even as Sevina strolled forward and toed it out of his reach.

"The decree has been made. No challenges will be met." She kicked the stone toward me. "And you, Ruby Morvannon, are not of the Nocturnes any longer."

As she turned away, dismissing me, I stepped into her path. She gave me a look that, in another time, might have cowed me. But I'd been away for a long time, and I'd lost my fear and almost every other emotion the moment she banished me.

"Then you will pay me for this male," I said, thrusting my chin upward. My wings flapped out, an impressive display, I could tell by the way her eyes traced their outline.

She eyed me, lip curling. "Ever the mercenary, Ruby Morvannon. Have you no care for your sisters or the survival of the Nocturnes?"

I ran my hand over the blade sheathed on my thigh. Not a threat. Just a reminder that I'd been a killer for hire only because she had made it necessary. When her gaze trailed to the weapon, I thought I saw her face blanch.

"My care is for my blood-born sister, Madre." My feet spread apart, planting themselves as if ready to do battle. "Now that I am no longer of the Nocturnes I owe them nothing."

Sevina crossed her arms. "Perhaps you should have shown that care the day you killed her."

My breath caught in my chest, burning a hole there that spread to my belly and up my throat. It took effort to speak again, and when I did, the rage tasted vile and bilious.

"It was your single-minded focus on power that drove her to her death, not me. Enyali would never have left her temple, never gone out on raid, and never above ground, were you less fanatical about our sisters lineage and the magic they procured or birthed for the weave."

She was nonplussed in the face of my anger. "We need diverse powers. You know this. It has taken us generations to get where we are, and generations more to go before we have all the magic we need. If not for my single-minded fanaticism, we'd still be trows and trolls and shades of Aiofe's thralls."

I refused to budge even though Askrid came up beside Sevina and glared at me.

"You will not pass him from one female to another like a bone. If you will not let me challenge for him, then you will pay. It's as simple as that."

Stone shifted against the restraints, the hum of bone and magic punctuating the silence.

"A single winner is not in the Nocturnes best interest. We will not drive ourselves toward extinction because you lust after a male." She gestured at Stone. "While I can quicken the sisters' wombs, I can't guarantee daughters from the coupling. We must have multiple broodings."

I sucked the back of my teeth. "You mean you've lost the power to quicken reliably." I took a step toward her. "You're old, Madre. You're old and your own powers are waning and wasting. The last time your magics procured a brood of daughters you nearly wasted."

Her face turned blood red. "Hush," she yelled.

Askrid side-stepped into the space between us, blocking my view of the Madre. I had to look around her to speak to her.

"The times of conceiving are getting more rare," I said. "That's why you demanded Enyali's service. It's why she sought out the angel, to increase her chances of brooding a daughter with all the power you could hope for in the Nocturnes."

My breath was coming in gasps as the memory stole over me. I had to shove it down, just to focus on this one important thing.

"If you won't pay for the male, then let me offer you one more incentive."

I shouldered my way past Askrid, who refused to move and ended up butting bone into bone as we contacted. My sidelong glance at her, I hoped, was filled with malice. Whatever she saw on my face made her take a step sideways.

I ended up nearly nose to nose with Sevina. The smell of ozone was strong, but beneath it, there was a musty fragrance—of old earth and moldering leaves. From behind Sevina, Stone strained against the warriors holding him, but his gaze never left my face.

"I can offer you what you want most," I said.

"And what is that?" Her nostrils flared.

"A daughter of the line," I said. "My line. A line with the natal and innate magics to foresee the perfect males to add to our weave. One who can scry for the right timing, who can continue the line if need be."

The excitement in her eyes was sickening. "You have this knowledge? You see these things?" The hope in her voice that I might have enough of the seer magic to produce what she needed was almost too much.

I thrust my chin upward. "Much of it is in shadow," I said, not lying. "But my daughter will see more. Enyali told me this. Before she died."

Sevina swallowed, and I knew I had her. She was all but drooling at the thought of owning another powerful oracle.

"You've wanted this of me since Enyali died, before even. Something you asked of me dozens of times and I refused."

Her sharp intake of breath caught Askrid's attention, but Sevina ignored it. In her face, I saw all the greed of any low-born mortal hungry for immortality. She swallowed that light that glowed beneath the skin of her wrinkled face, doing her best to hide it from me. The tilt of her head showed a sudden youth in those aged eyes.

It was too late. I'd seen it, and she knew it.

"Yes," I said, nodding. "I will surrender to the Quickening."

The Sisters were not prone to revealing their emotions, and yet a massive gasp, a collective inhalation that sounded almost comical except that I could see every single face in the torchlight.

I knew she wanted me to choose first. Her every muscle showed it. But whichever I chose, she and the Nocturnes would win. If Stone seeded even one of the Sisters during the long-night, it would be seen as a win.

Her gaze flicked to my piece of bone, that wrist bone I'd taken from a young fae so many years earlier. He'd had the softest hair. A shade of silver reminiscent of tarnished metal. Eyes to match with a black center and a circle of bright silver. But he was considered ugly for a fae. Wiry and stringy like he'd never battled so much as a single fly in his days.

He hadn't struggled. While the other Morrakai had to subdue their quarry, mine had come willingly. One look at the Sisters of Shadow and the shimmering skin that made them beautiful no matter what form they took, and he asked only if he might do what he wanted with them.

I watched Sevina's gaze skim the surface of that wrist bone, and though I wasn't good at reading emotions. I understood from her face that she was calculating the cost of this decision.

It had been long since anyone had brought a male of this strength and power, no matter what his natals were. She wanted this for the Nocturnes.

But was keeping him worth the risk of losing potentially many more Sisters with new, blended powers, for the hope of gaining a new seer for the Nocturnes? There was no guarantee I'd bear a seer. But she'd tired of living and raiding without insight.

I saw all that in her face as I watched her, and I thought of Enyali's sacrifice to the Nocturnes weave. She'd tempted an angel to get more magic, and it cost her life. She'd argued to keep me out of the Castings because my moment and what it might bear hadn't yet come.

But was this that moment?

My lips curled as I watched these calculations play out over The Madre's face. The sisters were getting restless as they stood around us. Stone, now sitting trussed up and glowering, looked violent.

She had to make a decision. I stood my ground; the bone gripped tightly in my fist. Head high, I held her gaze until she pulled hers away first.

"Did you hear me, Sevina?" I held my breath, waiting, the bone digging into my palm.

Finally, she growled beneath her breath, and I knew I'd won. My breath leaked from me in a hiss.

"You may have him, then, if you wish to claim him," she snapped, and her dismissive gesture drew a howl of outrage from Askrid.

The sisters began keening in loud clicks and snaps. The chaos was enough to gutter the torches and send wafts of mist up around Stone's shoulders.

Sevina held up her hand. The chaos grew louder still until she yelled to the circle. "Enough."

Even so, it still took a long time for the chaos to settle and the cacophony to quiet.

The Madre crossed her arms over her chest, making herself look broader, meaner, and while I'd seen that sort of Spartan command on her face dozens of times in the past, I was almost afraid of it right then. I knew my victory was a sacrificial one.

She faced me, and her gaze hardened. "You may have him this long night," she said. "But you will give us the daughter you bear. She will belong to the Nocturnes. She and her powers. And then you will leave the Nocturnes forever."

She jerked her chin at Stone. "The male will remain. And when all is done, he will succumb to the blooding. And if you do not quicken," she said., "your sisters will deliver you to Aiofe's Kumara along with this male and we will make our own vow with the queen of darkness for his death."

She squinted at me.

"Or you may simply leave him to the sisters now and let his soul find the queen's throne room in its own time."

She gave me a canny look. "Your choice, Morvannon. You could be free to go."

Free to go. Meaning I could save myself and leave Stone to the Nocturnes and hope his death would be enough for Aiofe to relinquish her hold on my sister. The only one in my entire life who cared what happened to me.

Free to go and continue my long life without my sister, without my mate.

I could leave the Nocturnes and remain alive, but alone, for centuries more.

The entire world of the Nocturnes seemed to hold its breath along with me. We all knew that promise would gain him nothing but a few spare hours. I was a mercenary. I'd been one for decades already, and if I agreed, I could be one for generations more. All for the price of relinquishing the progeny of a mate who loathed me.

I couldn't look at Stone. My chest hurt just thinking about him. My fingers itched to slap the cunning smirk from the Madre's face.

My mouth was almost too dry to speak, but I knew the Madre's greed. I knew the withering of the Nocturnes and their need for more magic. I understood the lengths they would go to obtain another of the seer line if Enyali should indeed be lost to them.

And I made a decision. What was a mere unknown entity to me compared to the lifetime of my mate?

"His life is mine," I said calmly.

She shook her head, not convinced. My chin thrust upward as I locked onto her gaze.

"When this is over, you may have the daughter, but his life belongs to me."

"You would risk your sister's life for a male? You would risk your own life?"

I looked at Sevina, and I let her see the level of my fear and the truth of it.

"I'm risking nothing," I murmured. "I have lived decades already without love. My sister is already lost. And if the Morrakai take from me my last breath and sends me to Kumara because I have not brought a daughter to the realm, then I would have at least had a moment of joy."

Stone snorted from his spot on the ground, and I refused to look at him. He would fight, I knew, and the Madre could take from him his surrender with her herbs and magic. I wouldn't have to feel his hatred.

But though I felt his energy rising, I knew he wouldn't argue now. He understood what was happening. That I was bidding for his life in those moments. He would accept it because it gave him hours more to plot and plan his escape and kill me somewhere, sometime, in the daylight realms.

That was fine. I would have saved him, and it would be worth it.

I squared my shoulders. My wings dipped behind me, touching the earth and bolstering me as I faced the Madre.

"Pool your power and concentrate it on one womb," I said to her, my heart aching over the choice I was making. "Let this one male live after the Quickening this one time in all our centuries for the good of the realm."

Her mouth twitched. I saw her glance at Askrid. She wanted this. But she could yet defer to the Morraka. will and cast Stone to the mercy of the warriors.

"As long as I live," I said, spreading my palm toward her to distract her, to press her toward the thing she really wanted. "I vow not to challenge you over the fruit of this union and to never return for her."

"Then say the words, Morvannon," Sevina said, her eyes shuttering cunningly.

Inhaling deeply through my nose, I closed my eyes. "I claim this male for the Nocturnes," I intoned. "I give my womb in service to the darkness."

Stone went still at the intonation, his expression unreadable, the air between us tightening like a drawn bowstring. Even so, I kept on.

"I ask the power of the Madre to quicken my blood and flow and bring down the magic of life."

Sacred as the words were, I didn't get more than an instant of peace before Askrid launched herself at me.

Chapter 14

I'D MENTORED UNDER ASKRID for two decades before I'd ever been able to stand against her. That moment was burned in my memory because she never played or fought honestly. She was the one who taught me to distract an opponent by feigning an injury. When they thought they'd marked you, they let their guard down. Not for long, but just enough to slide your killing thrust into the fight. But you had to be quick. You had to know what to look for.

Askrid didn't wait for me to finish my sentence before she struck out.

But it was Stone who blocked the spear. At some point during the drama, he'd risen to his feet. While everyone else, including Askrid, was focused on the drama unfolding between us, he was watching my mentor. So when she attacked, he was ready.

His forearm knocked her wrist, driving the blade upward. In a motion so fast it took my breath away, he had twisted into her body, throwing her off balance and onto his back.

He heaved her the way a bear might throw off a badger from its back. She landed several paces away, hard enough that a moan escaped her.

But he wasn't done. He came for me next. Already aimed in my direction, it took a breath and no more before he was on me. Of course he'd turn on me; saving me hadn't been mercy; it had been strategy. I was the next predator in line.

I knew he didn't expect me to parry his blow as fast as he launched it. Hand to hand combat hadn't been my true forte for decades, but I'd done plenty enough over my lifetime that the cell memory was still there. I blocked and ducked out of reach even though the sudden movement cost me in sharp intakes of breath.

I danced out of his way, but he was like a big cat pissed at being bothered from its siesta. The way he slunk about, almost liquid in his movements, he was everywhere and right there as if his body was a long, slinking thing, when it was obvious he was a burly, square-shouldered male.

It took focus to stay out of his way. Despite his own injuries, his exhaustion from beating back the sisters, he moved quickly. While he had speed and brawn on his side, I had the magics that let me slide in and out of the Nocturnes into another realm. I could be shadow and solid at the same time, and he found it impossible to land a blow.

I halted at one point, just out of reach, when he'd thrown an exhausted punch and missed.

The injuries were getting the better of him, I could tell, but when he caught my eye and his lip curled back, he could put all his loathing into his words.

"I am no fae's plaything," he growled. "I fuck who I want. I am not fucked."

A laugh bubbled free. "Trust me, Stone. We are both fucked here."

I side-stepped as he threw another punch. I tried my best to move without falling into the straddling line between realms, not wanting to use too much source. But there were times when I had no choice. He was too fast. Too strong, even though his weariness lay like a heavy cloak over his shoulders.

And yet, there was joy in the battle. In the sensation that I could release my guilt and regret. The feeling that he relished the chance to vent his frustration and rage.

My sisters held back, watching. I felt their eyes on us, rabid almost for the energy that each attack and advance and avoidance created. An almost palpable energy, like a miasma settling down over their shoulders.

The circle pulsed, sisters shifting in and out like a breathing organism

At one point, he paused and canted his head at me. I let myself seep back into the solid plane and ran my gaze over his entire body. He didn't seem winded. There was no anger in his posture. More a plodding, calculating wonder.

"Use your magics," I said, lifting my chin. I felt like he was testing me physically, and I sensed he was gauging my powers before using his. "What's stopping you?"

"You know why," he said, his head dropping so that he looked more bullish than catlike.

Truth was something the fae understood in ways that were complex and complete. He understood more than I thought and knew that to reveal himself and his magics here might do more harm than good.

He wasn't wrong.

"I do know," I said, annoyed to hear the breathiness in my voice. Even if my powers sourced from the Nocturnes, the control of the eddy, the aerobics of ducking and parrying, was exhausting my physical body. "Which is why you need to stop. Now."

He snorted. "I will stop fighting when I'm dead."

The sisters snickered. I barely cast a glance at the ones behind his back. I couldn't risk taking my eyes off him. Not seeing how fast he was. Not after he'd tossed the strongest of us over his shoulder like a rag.

Stone, however, seemed to think he had all the leisure to study them in the flickering torchlight. I could almost see him counting out the forms he saw surrounding us. Every subtle play of his gaze on each form was a calculation.

That was the moment I knew it wasn't about survival or rage at all. He was too methodical. Too calm.

It was a quiet noting of each sister. Their height. Their flares of magic as the energy seeped out of them. It was the way he studied the temple facade, how far it was from Sevina as she stepped backward to give us room to fight.

And that was when I realized he wasn't looking for escape routes. He was counting how many sisters would take their turn after me. Because he didn't trust me. He could never trust me.

For him, there was no meaningful difference between the sisters and me. I was merely the one who delivered him. The one who would take him first before passing him along like the rest.

Every torch. Every shadow. Every distance between bodies. He was preparing himself for the moment they drugged him because he believed no one was going to save him.

A single glance at one of my sisters, facing me with a look of awe on her face as she took in the broad, gorgeous shape of the fae whose fists were curled at his sides.

They wanted him. There was no doubt. And knowing he was playing them gave me the courage to stand down. I dropped my arms. My wings folded over my back and cupped my ribs like an embrace.

"What are your innate magics, Stone?" I asked. "Why did Aiofe want you dead?"

His eyebrows rose in concert with the shocked expressions of my sisters.

"I know your father's natal magics," I advanced more, watching his eyes closely in case they revealed an intention to attack again. "Terran of the Sentinels. Captain of the Prince's Guard. He abandoned his post just as the prince rose to the Iron Kingdom's throne. Like us here in the Nocturnes, he's not really high fae, is he? Just a baser creed whose magics are animalistic. Strong. Fast. Transformation magic." .

I could draw this out as long as he could, if it meant I had a chance of convincing him of my sincerity. Whatever he needed to believe in me, I would give him the time to gain it.

I stopped four paces away, and he'd watched every single move I'd made. Each swing of my arms, he took in. He measured each step with a flick of his gaze. The way he mirrored my movements with the most subtle movements of his fingers told me he'd memorized my gait and where I leaned slightly.

I doubted he noticed me noticing these things. His cataloging of these small things that could give him an edge took all his focus.

"You see, I do my research," I said. "I know you would have been granted some of those powers as part of your natal weave. I don't have to guess which ones. But your mother's line was hidden. High fae and yet no real history."

A muscle near his ear tightened and went white.

My sisters closed the circle with a single pace. I felt the energy running through them as if they were a single wire. Sevina's gaze sharpened, and I knew he saw it because his shoulders squared.

His hands dropped to his sides, and all struggle went out of his body. His eyes flicked to the sisters behind me. Not with longing, but calculation.

"If we're to fuck," he said in a long, heaving sigh. "Then let's get to it."

I blinked at the abrupt change. My jaw ticked to the side. I felt like I was being led into a trap but couldn't see the blind or the bait. I pivoted, daring to put my back to him, and scanned the circle.

That was when I noticed Sevina's guarded expression as she shot a warning look at Askrid. The Morrakai had edged in closer during the battle, no doubt drawn by the energy of violence. But there was more, and that was the thing that made my stomach roll.

Askrid stood closer than them all, flanked by three of her favorites. A glance told me she'd been about to launch her own attack. At me.

It was only Stone's surrender that halted it. Without the distraction, Askrid had no cover.

And Sevina had seen it just in time, her warning look holding them back just in time.

Stone had seen it while I hadn't. He'd read their intent and submitted.

I felt an electric hum along my spine, rising like a serpent to coil around my throat. I couldn't speak because of the ache that gripped my voice box. And even if I could, it wouldn't matter.

The time for reprieve was over.

Sevina raised her arms and emitted a note so shrill that the ghost pipe in her hands trembled and wilted, then liquefied into an iridescent pool that hovered over her head.

The mist that had been welling up curled along her calves and thighs all the way to her fingertips and transformed into a goblet of amber crystal.

I'd seen the sight before, of course, but it always sent a sharp pain through my solar plexus, the same as it did to every Morrakai standing in the circle.

Each of us gasped in shock and sudden, unexpected pain, and a tug very much like a thread being pulled through the muscle of my heart made me lift up onto my toes.

For a moment, I couldn't breathe.

The magics of the ritual began in earnest, drawing from each of us and pouring from the shadows into the goblet like mist in reverse.

And when the goblet was filled to overflowing, Sevina closed the distance between herself and Stone. She lifted the cup to his mouth.

"Drink," she said to Stone.

His shoulders squared, and his back straightened. I thought he would knock the chalice from her hands, but he locked his eyes on mine and took it from her instead.

Draining it, his eyes never wavered from mine, peering over the brim with an intensity that felt like the sun burning through my retinas.

And then all was blackness for a very long time.

I'd never known the fullness of the ritual, though I'd seen it in the others. I'd been one of the few who did the ritual bathing. The anointing of magiced oils. I'd dressed the youth of my choosing all those years ago in a kilt of linen and drawn runes on his skin. I'd washed my sisters with scented water and smudged their bellies with night sage and dressed them in loose shifts of water silk so sheer their navels held the only secret.

All while those complied with an almost blind and numb affect. Some said they swam in the rivers of Aiofe's Styx. Some swore they rested like babes in the fabrics of a lush blanket. For the time when the magic took them, they appeared to be sleepwalking.

The sacrificial males didn't enjoy the same. They were prodded and tested and taunted and forced to rise and fall so they would be mad with lust when they were herded to their places of bedding.

Whatever happened to me in those moments of darkness, I only knew his eyes when I returned to the realm, aware and starving for his touch.

My belly warmed. A husky, smoky heat coiled up my throat at the sight of him. They'd dressed him in the typical kilt, and his body, bare from the hips up, truly did look like it was carved from some glorious stone. He'd been washed of blood and cleaned of wounds. One of the sisters with healing magic had knitted his abrasions and cuts.

He looked even more magnificent than he had the moment I'd first seen him in his own daylight realm.

"Come to me, Stone of Terran," I said in a voice that didn't sound remotely like my own. To my ears, it sounded like a blend of every sister of the Morrakai, a lilting, swollen sound. "It is time."

I held out my hand. I was close enough that he could use it to subdue me in any number of ways, but the energy of the circle had shifted and time was running down. I had no choice but to risk pushing him to make a decision.

"Let me take you to the temple," I said. I wasn't sure how I knew, but I was sure they'd prepared the sanctuary for us, and it couldn't have held a better omen.

I waggled one finger, the way I would to a squirrel I was trying to encourage into my palm so I could save an arrow on a meal.

His eyes flickered down to my outstretched palm, and I held my breath. The whole situation could turn on half a heartbeat.

"Please," I said. I doubted he expected me to beg and by then I didn't care. Soft clicking sounds had begun to move through the circle, encouragement from the sisters. They'd lost, but they had hopes of winning something more.

Sevina drew up to her full height, but yet somehow, still looked hunched and shriveled. I recalled her own bone cast into the lot and tried to imagine her with Stone. If nothing else, I'd spared him that.

My head hung as she shouted loud enough to startle the bats from the roof of the temple.

"She of the Morvannon has cast and won."

Her gaze trailed from face to face and settled on mine. The look in her eyes told me she understood something I didn't want to believe. That while I had saved him from being assaulted by a dozen violent Sidhe females, I knew that I'd doomed him to intimacy with a female he loathed.

And I was sure it would break him.

Chapter 15

When the sisters dragged Stone to the temple, I was sure he would fight back. He didn't. And that both mollified and terrified me. The powerful male, who had done everything he could to resist, had fallen beneath the power and magics of the potion, and a small part of me grieved.

Sevina followed along behind the train of Sisters as we entered the temple. She placed a fragrant goblet on the altar. The liquid inside looked crimson and lit from below. I noted his gaze pinned to it in the same way a wounded man looked at ale.

With a wave of her hand, she called her magic to conjure a soft animal fur to cover the floor, a roaring fire in the scrying bowl that somehow grew to dimensions that would rival a broad stone hearth.

It crackled with an ominous intensity, bringing beads of sweat to my brow.

She turned to me. "The ghost pipe has done its work in letting us prepare him. It has created in him a desire for more so that when it begins to wear thin, he will want more." Her head angled toward the goblet. "The rest is up to you."

She didn't need to issue a threat or a reminder of what was at stake if I failed to bring Stone to the furs. She merely gestured to the Morrakai who had followed her in, and together they threaded their way back through the copper door, leaving us alone.

My core trembled. The ritual bath, the sumptuous feel of cool silk against my skin, the feel of the cold flagstones on my bare feet, all seemed surreal. But the knowledge that I was about to force myself on an unwilling mate ruined all the pleasure of those sensations.

I swallowed through a tight throat as I stepped around him to the altar.

"It might be easier on you if you drink the potion," I said, lifting the goblet into the space between us.

He eyed it with some suspicion. "They have a saying in the human realms. *Never drink or eat of anything offered by the fae*. We have a similar saying for the Sidhe."

I nodded. "And yet you drank of Sevina's potion outside."

He grinned suddenly, a heart-stopping smile filled with the wry humor I'd seen during his times escorting the mortal women.

"You're awfully naive for a mercenary."

I snuffed air through my nose. Whatever he'd seemed, the ghost pipe had not dulled his calculating mind.

"You didn't drink it at all," I guessed.

He shrugged. "My brother Blade told me once...always make sure the snake is tossed into the fire."

"You let them think you drank it."

His fingers stroked his chin. "I let them believe I drank it because that was what they wanted. And I learned a lot about your world, Ruby Morvannon."

My mouth twisted at the confession. The thought of him standing docilely by while the sisters prepared him, touched him, burned in my gut.

"Even so," I said. "You might want to now. At least you'd be spared full knowledge of what you're doing."

I licked my lips and offered it again. "It's the best I can do for you."

He pushed the cup away and sat on the edge of the altar with one foot planted to keep himself balanced. He looked casual. Unafraid as he raked his hand over his short-cropped hair. The linen kilt buckled over his hips, and I had to fight the urge to travel that line of muscle and curve. The magics of the Quickening were growing more insistent.

"You already did the best you could do for me," he whispered. "And at great risk to yourself."

"There is no risk," I said. "I meant every word."

He gestured to the empty spot beside him. It was still smeared with dust. A pang of grief hit me as I thought of the sister who would have kept this place sacred.

"If you don't conceive, they will have your life in forfeit."

"It isn't much of a life anymore," I said, and perched on the corner, far enough away that I wouldn't touch him, giving him space. With a sigh, I let the cup rest on my lap. The drink inside smelled sweet and faintly of barley and shadow cherries. The bitter tang of ghost pipe hidden beneath the cloying palate of fruit.

I felt him adjust himself on the surface, relaxing onto the stone. "You did all this for your sister," he said.

I nodded, though I didn't have to. "At first, yes." Stealing a glance sideways, I wrapped my palms around the goblet. "She was my reason for tracking you. But not the reason I brought you here." It was hard, that confession. I'd not realized it at the time, but the strong desire to hold on to him had everything to do with what he had come to mean to me.

"When did you first realize I was your mate?" he asked.

The question left me gawking at him. "You know?"

He sighed heavily. "I've known since the moment you shot the blade out of Irina's hand."

My throat felt too thick, too tight to swallow. He'd known. All along, he'd known and hadn't given a hint of realization. This Stone was far more practiced in cunning than I'd realized.

It wasn't common for a fae to reject their mate. Certainly, it happened when the pair were ignorant of each other. But to flat-out reject it took deep emotion.

I understood the depth of his hatred then. I ran my thumb over the rim of the goblet. I couldn't force him to drink it, knowing that. And I couldn't force him to go through with the rites.

And yet, I could think of no way out for either of us.

"That's why you spared me," he said, cutting through the awful miasma of thought. "Though I know it confused you at the time. And when you ran that blade over my throat..." he chuckled, a deep throaty sound that hinted at a base sense of humor. "Well, I can't say I was expecting that."

His laughter, however brief, was a balm. It relieved the ache, if only for a moment.

"I was blood bound," I said. "I swore to bring you to your death so my sister could live again, free of Aiofe's thrall."

He leaned back, edging just a little closer. "I was relieved when Nutkin saved me," he said in a musing tone. "Now I'm not so sure."

My turn to laugh, this time humorlessly. "Whatever you face here with me, has to be better than facing Aiofe and a lifetime in Kumara, don't you think?"

"Is it really so bad for your sister?"

"The legends about the Queen of the Stygian Darkness pale in comparison to the truth. Enyali cannot regain her magics," I said. "Aiofe siphons it as quickly as it grows, the same as her other thralls. She is greedy for power. Almost as though she's hemorrhaging it."

The thought of Aiofe using my sister to gather yet more power was enough to force me to my feet. I placed the goblet on the altar beside him and spun to step away. Everything was coming to a head. Too much emotion. Too many conflicting, powerful feelings threatened to overcome me even as the vow I'd made to my sisters seemed impossible.

His nearness felt both too much and not enough. I wanted to slide into his arms and let him wrap his arms around me, and yet I knew he wouldn't. The urge and the sensation of being rejected were too much. I couldn't just sit there, bowing beneath the weight of the adrenaline and fear.

His hand clamped down around my wrist just as I stood. The fingers curled tightly, his thumb pressing down on my pulse. I felt the hammering of it against his skin in echo and looked down at him.

A flare moved through his gaze, smoldering. Filled with the promise of magic and peace, but also swirling with high emotions, the same as me.

"And your own Madre has no greed of power?"

"She wears the weighty cloak of our survival," I said, hating my defense of her. "We are bound to the source until we gain enough magic, enough versatility to move beyond the darkness." The envy in my voice probably sounded bitter, but it wasn't. It was resignation.

"You can't know the ache of wanting to live in the light," I said. "The sisters have evolved to live in darkness but it hasn't been easy. Bringing light into the Nocturnes is a strain. So much that we don't bother with it most times."

"That's why the noises," he murmured, but he didn't let go of my wrist. "It's how you all see."

"It saves energy," I said. "But it's not how I see." Did I want to confess just how clear my vision was? That my magics allowed me that freedom when I had no liberation in any other area?

For a moment, we stayed like that. His fingers curled around my wrist, my pulse throbbing against the pad of his thumb, both of us looking into each other's eyes. My throat ached at the way his face looked. My insides felt as though the entire Morrakai were emitting pulses of echolocation, the noises striking chords in my tissues as they sought the light, sought freedom.

And then it was too much. I couldn't just stand there, waiting for something that was not going to happen. I tried to pull away, using the leverage of my body to free myself. I expected him to release me, grateful himself to be free of me.

But he pulled me closer. He dropped my hand against his chest, right over his heart. The soft machine inside ticking away in perfect time at first, then speeding up, matching my own.

"You feel that?" he asked.

Mere words seemed impossible as a response. I nodded.

"We are in rhythm," he murmured. "I feel your pain. I know the beat of your heart. I know the taste of your breath though I've never kissed you. Is it the same for you?"

The mate bond, trying to make itself known. I wasn't sure why that broke me, but it did.

"And you hate that it's so," I said, terrified that he would realize that the bond was not unwanted on my end. I did want him. Despite every alarm bell, every instinct that told me it would be a bad thing, I wanted him very much.

He rose from his planted perch on the altar stone and stepped into my space. His breath, like honey and caramel, promised a sweetness I didn't deserve as it gathered over my brow. My guts coiled at the worry that he was about to tell me I was right. That he hated the bond and would reject it. That the act we performed would mean nothing to him when I so badly wanted it to be the opposite. With not a single prescient bone in my body to confirm the opposite, impossible hope flared.

And that hope terrified me. I couldn't bear to let it be dashed so soon. I had to reject it for him, find every reason for him to do it so it wouldn't hurt so much.

So I stood an instant after he did and found a spot at the edge of the fur skin to stand upon. Far enough away that his eyes wouldn't capture me. I toed the edge of the lovely fur sewn together with golden thread and wanted him to truly know the depths of the horrors he was about to succumb to. Because that was the only way I could dampen the pain.

"There has never been a match of love here in the Nocturnes. We take a male's seed and we dispose of the remains." I paced from side to side of the fur skin laid over a good distance of the dais, gaining space from him but too drawn to completely move away. "I killed many fae in my time. Some were burned alive. Others flayed and consumed."

I halted dead center, directly across from him, my jaw jutting out, daring him to see the horrors of the Nocturnes in my words and declare it too violent. He merely drew his hands over his hips and clasped them, drawing more ire from somewhere in my solar plexus.

"We've sent male infants to the Darkness," I declared. "Each of them borne to this realm given to Aiofe to use as she would."

I held my breath. Chin thrust upward, eyes level. Let him make of that what he would.

"We are not a world of light and love," he said. "Our realms are similar in violence. My father's own tutor uses human women as portals to their realm. We of the Iron Kingdom have murdered and consumed our own share of unfortunates."

When a premature gasp clung to my lips, I held it back. But he noticed and grappled for my hand across the fur, taking a step I didn't see him take to do so.

"The worlds of the fae are complex and not all powered by light, Ruby," he said and the sound of my name on his lips made me hold my breath, trying to savor it. "I have dark secrets of my own to atone for. We are not so unalike," he said. "We both feel the power of an unwanted bond..."

"We are not the same," I said, trying again to pull away. "We are nothing alike. You are good. Light. You're the breath of a dawn morning in the summer courts. I'm nothing but a smudge of shadow."

His chuckle was exactly that, and I hated the way it warmed my insides, despite knowing...knowing that he was mocking me. But then he pulled me against his chest, his arms going round me like a vise.

Broad hands cupped my ribs. "You make me sound like something from a dream," he said and bent his head to my hair. It took everything in me not to lift my face to that mouth. I went rigid with the fight against the urge.

And yet, even as every muscle in my body tensed, waiting for the inevitable rejection, he softened against me, molding himself to my body in ways that made me shiver.

"I won't pretend this is the way I would have wanted to bed my mate for the first time," he said. "I would not choose to be forced. But you risked much to save my life. You have a hellhound's vigor and a kitten's heart."

"I know this is something you have to do to save your own skin," I said. "Take the potion." I angled toward the goblet still on the altar. "It won't remove your hatred of me, but it will remove the distaste the way sugar removes astringent. Take it," I took his hand and examined the calluses in the firelight. "Let it give you that escape."

His finger crooked beneath my chin, drawing my face toward his gaze. "Fuck the potion," he said, his voice gritty and husky. "I won't let myself be spelled to compulsion. When I touch you, you will know that every stroke, every kiss, is intentional. Desired. Wanted."

I swallowed. His words raised a painful, sharp and unwanted hope.

"You...you want me?" I was almost afraid to hear his answer.

His silence was painful. "I did," he finally said. "Before I knew what you were."

"I'm a monster," I said, agreeing.

He sat down on the altar. His hands slid to my hips before I realized he meant to pull me onto his lap.

"I am not blind. Beauty is beauty and I don't see a monster. I wanted you then, yes. Very much."

"And now?" I held my breath as his thighs shifted beneath me, parting mine with quiet command.

His forehead dipped to lie against mine. I felt the pressure the way one might feel pushing against the stone of a great mountain.

"What I want now is different," he said, his breath whispering over my cheeks. "It's raw and angry. The bond is overlaid with violence and vengeance. What might have been true and gentle at one time has now transformed the way light changes the shapes of shadow. It's hard and sharp instead of blunted by mystery and curiosity."

The bond thrummed between us—alive, angry. Every beat of his heart called to mine, and my body betrayed me, curving around his as if it couldn't stand a breath of air.

"But it is powerful, Ruby." He looked deep into my eyes. "And I can't deny it. There's something beneath that bond that speaks to me the way a firefly signals in the darkness to find the same signal in return."

A stroke of his finger across my cheek made my eyes flutter upward to see his gaze boring into me. "I can't promise to be gentle. My rage may overtake me. My sense of vengeance. The resentment for the slash of your blade on my throat. For bringing me here."

My eyes closed, trying to shut out the memory if not the intensity of the emotion in his gaze. And when I did, I felt his lips on my eyelids, not a kiss, but a whisper of touch so compassionate that water burned beneath the skin.

"But know this. I do want you. I want to see the light in your eyes when I bury my cock inside you. I want to hear you moan. I want to hear you whisper my true name and find it dripping with desire."

I opened my eyes finally to see that he still had his gaze locked on mine.

A smile played over his mouth, crinkling the corners of his eyes. "I want all of those things and I hate myself for it at the same time. Can't that be enough?"

I sighed, and even though I wanted nothing more than to sag into his embrace, I slid free of his lap. He remained on the altar, giving me space as I stepped back, the heat from the fire a shivering line down my spine.

"Because you don't love me," I said. I'd known this would be about duty, maybe even desire, but I wasn't sure that was all I wanted. All I needed.

"Is it really love you feel for me?" he asked in a quiet voice.

His question was his answer, and it was so plain to me that I knew I should keep my own confession sealed behind caged lips and a blackened heart.

And yet I couldn't hold the truth at bay. In the magic of the temple, with the sacred energies already coiling around us, the words came whether I wanted them to or not. And they flooded the space in the same way light bent the blur of shadow into true shape.

"I've never known love except for my sister," I said. "I just know that this is an urge beyond my reasoning that compels me to break vows I made in secret. A desire beyond that of seeing my most beloved sister again." I slipped my hand in his and dropped my gaze to my feet because I couldn't say the next words and look into his face when I did so.

"It's a drive so powerful that I ache as if you were a limb severed from my body and I would do anything to have you back again."

My voice broke on the last words, and he gathered me into his embrace. The power of his body was evident in every fibre of muscle that lay against mine.

"Then we are indeed in rhythm, Ruby," he said. "This isn't the way I would want to woo a mate," he said. "But if it's the way we must meet then so be it. We have been cracked in so many ways, but not broken. Here, I can be yours and you can be mine. For these moments, the bond can be the gold that seals the cracks in our magic."

Chapter 16

With a long sigh, I extracted the bone I'd plucked from the earth's floor before entering the temple. It sat in my palm for a long moment. I didn't need the golden light of the pillar candles to see the etchings I'd carved into the surface. I traced the marks with my thumb, hearing Enyali's voice again as she bid me etch them into the surface on a night when the sisters had glutted themselves on sex and blood. We'd sat cross-legged together in the rooms off to the side of the temple, the place where she rested or prepared for long sessions of premonition.

Every single one of those marks was done at her instruction: a spell, she said. One of primitive words long before the language of either fae or human. Something to be cast when I knew the time was right.

I peered up at Stone. The cut of his hair, cropped close but still lush looking, made his jaw look strong and square. Cut from stone, Aiofe had said, and she was right. He fit into the surroundings the way a carved statue of a god might.

I turned and dropped the bone into the scrying bowl, now empty of water and filled instead with flame that licked upward greedily. At once, a plume of golden smoke lifted from the well. It curled above the altar and took shape.

If Stone recognized the form of a falcon, he said nothing, but he gasped when the smoke changed again to trace the outline of a mouse in the air.

It changed a third time, separating and twisting until it became both predator and prey. I didn't even gasp when the mouse reared up and swallowed the bird whole. I expected it.

He came up next to me. I felt him inhale, pause as if he wanted to speak.

"A falcon is the shape I'm meant to be," I said. "But here in the darkness, we are none of us the things we should be."

A small pivot of my feet and I was facing him. Breathing was like trying to inhale fire. "The other was the sigil of the boy I murdered."

His eyes narrowed. "For a moment, I thought you were mocking me with your magic."

I smiled, but there was no humor in it. "I'm afraid it's me the ivory mocks," I said. "The great bird bested in the end by the mouse it hunted. A fitting metaphor, is it not?"

His hand came up, slow and deliberate, his thumb hooking beneath my chin. "Then tonight, I'll be the mouse to your bird of prey," he murmured, voice low enough to tremble the air. "I've long wondered how falcon would taste on my tongue."

The words and emotion in it, the promise swelling beneath each syllable, robbed my knees of strength. A stutter ran through my heart, shooting lightning into my pulse.

He steadied me with gentle hands, seeming to sense the utter collapse of my will, then he pulled me away from the altar and onto the fur that lay on the floor.

We stood there awkwardly for an instant. The candles cast strong shapes against the stone walls even as they cast a glow that made him look like a haloed god.

The fur beneath my feet cushioned sound. The light radiated warmth. His breath drew me in warm as honey-suckled air.

"I don't know what to do," I confessed, the shame warming my cheeks.

Violence had been the only language I'd spoken. Tenderness was a foreign thing, and Stone's patient guidance dissolved the hard edges of my shame the way sunlight bleached bone.

His voice grew soft, patience a shadowed under-painting to the color of his usual tone. "Then start here," he said, taking my hand and holding it against his chest. "Map my body with your touch. Show me the terrain of yours. The rest will come."

From beneath his palm, my fingers trembled and then came to life, dancing to the drum of his heartbeat as it called me home. I roamed his chest, feeling the hardness of his muscles beneath his skin. With each inch I traced, his breath grew rougher. When my thumb found the hollow of his collarbone, he sucked in a sharp breath.

I peered up at him.

His eyelids were shuttered, but I could see him looking at me.

"Take your time, Ruby," he said.

"Ruvienne," I whispered. The admission felt dangerous and sacred at the same time. "My true name. I want to hear it on someone else's lips. Just once."

In response, his arm hooked around my waist and drew me flush against him until all the space that remained between us was our shared breath.

"Ruvienne," he murmured. "Perfect for you. Strong. Mysterious."

The way the word sounded on his tongue was like being released from a dark cage where every breath was a smothering struggle. The sensation of his breath sighing from his nostrils as he nuzzled beneath my chin to plant his lips against the pulse that hammered there sent my pulse into rapid fire.

"You're trembling," he said against my throat.

I looked at my fingers. They trembled as they touched his skin. "I've done horrible things with these hands."

I waited for him to flinch. Instead, he held my shaking fingers as if they had never slid a blade across a young fae's throat or stripped it of flesh. As if gentleness was their natural state.

The contradiction, the impossibility of it, made my breath hitch.

"Are you afraid, Ruvienne? Is it too much to trust me with all the power you have given me?"

Another pleasant thrill ran down my back at the way my name sounded on his breath. One that nearly stole all the air from my lungs.

"No." It was the only word I could manage through the pained tightness of my throat. But in that one word I gave every truthful thing in me, even though I couldn't voice the liberation, the joy of hearing him speak my name. That one word was everything I had.

His hands pressed into the small of my back, curving me even more into his body. My head fell back, and he roamed my skin with his mouth, breathing my name in a miasma of honey and caramel, making me drunk without so much as tasting the flavors. I could barely think anymore. I just knew the fabric between us was too much, and I started to peel the tunic from my shoulders without bothering to unlace the leather corset.

He widened his stance. "Let me," he said.

And then he was undressing me, taking his time with every inch of material, kissing the skin as the fabric peeled away. In agonizingly languid measures, he tasted my body, warming my skin with his breath as the chilled air caressed me and brought gooseflesh to the surface.

His hands trailed a long journey along my spine, taking their time with each vertebra as though he would drum something sacred from each before moving to the next.

He was methodical but not clinical with his touch, drawing little sounds from me that I'd be ashamed of later. I felt his smile against my flesh each time a noise of frustration or pleasure escaped me, and for some reason that made me more excited.

Sometimes his breath tickled. Other times, it made me claw for the knot tying his kilt, eager to touch him the way he was touching me. Each time, he patiently corrected me, silently reclaiming control.

And when he finally had me freed of the wads of linen, he stood back and let his gaze travel the inches he'd already mapped. It was so intense, standing there nude, my hands crept to my hips, and only then, did he speak.

"Let me see you," he said, his voice husky and deep. "My breath already knows your body, Ruvienne. Let my eyes drink it in now."

It took an effort of will to lift my chin and drop my hands, but I forced myself to relent. My eyes shut, not able to bear seeing what he might think of the scars and the muscled stomach, the cords of sinew in my arms and legs. Not feminine. A body made for violence. A body so hard it lacked curves and shape.

A body, hands and feet and arms that had earned nothing but disgust. I braced for it, knowing that ever since that poor boy's blood drained at my touch, that revulsion was what I had earned.

He took in long drafts of air the way a man might before plunging into a pool of deep water, and I was certain he was bracing himself. And yet when I peeked open one eye, I saw a male mesmerized. His gaze was glued to the pulse in my throat.

"The altar," he said in a tight voice. "I want to take you there."

"It's sacred," I said, my voice a bit too timid.

"Fuck that," he said. "It's where you belong."

My expression must have shown my confusion, because he jerked his chin at the stone altar. "Get on it. Now."

He swallowed hard, and I made a move to lift the scrying bowl from its pedestal. I must have been moving too slow. With a grunt of impatience, he closed the distance between us in three paces, the fur catching on his bare feet. Ignoring it, he swept the bowl sideways, and it hung in the air perfectly balanced until it drifted to the floor without a sound.

Even before it landed, he'd hoisted me from my feet and planted me on the cold stone. The chill of the granite was a shock, but not unpleasant. His eyes searched my face, and the hunger in his gaze made my breath hitch, my chest ache.

"Spread your legs," he said.

They were already drifting apart anyway, drawing his gaze, which left his head tilted, revealing that thick bristle of hair that cried out for my fingers. I watched his head bob as he skimmed the inside of my thighs with a probing glance, and I thought I might evaporate.

It was his fingers that grounded me. They trailed to my hips as he nudged himself between my legs, measuring the space with his body, taking up every inch of room till I felt I'd never breathe again.

"Wider," he said, pushing closer, broadening my span with his hips and hands as they forced them further apart. "I want to see all of you, taste all of you. If I want to climb inside for fuck's sake, you'll make the room I need, do you hear me?"

My nod was silent because I couldn't find my voice. It was too strangled by the desire now coiling deep into the core of my stomach.

I fully expected him to bury himself inside me right then, but he dropped to his knees instead, and what he took from me in the next few moments left me trembling and limp. My throat hurt as though something raw had been dragged out of it.

When he lifted his head, chin glistening in the candlelight, I thought I might melt from the heat that swam over me. Heat wavered in the air, striping the chamber in color and shadow. It was only when I realized he was standing and gripping me by the hips with fingers that dug into my skin that I knew I was airborne.

My wings had spread and lifted me from the altar. I hovered in the air, the air currents billowing beneath my outstretched wings, Stone below me, looking up at me as though he was about to devour me.

"Come to me," he said, stretching his hand upward to rest on my ribs. "I won't cage you, pretty bird, but I would like to soar with you."

Without thinking, my wings folded back into place, and I dropped into his arms. He knelt, cradling me until we were on the fur, and laid me before him on its soft surface.

"You know what will happen when we join?" I asked, giving him one more chance to decide. If I had had to face the consequences of the Nocturnes, it would have been worth it for that one moment.

"I know well what you bargained for in return for my life," he said, his voice husky. "And I vow right here to free you of it once and for all."

When he gathered me into his arms again, I felt small enough to fit into the tiniest crack in a massive boulder, safe from the winds and rain. Darkness had no power in that space because there was only me. With no room for darkness or light, I felt like the kernel in a seed, protected until it found nourishment to grow.

And when he thrust into me, hard and violent, with a grunt that brought a gasp of pleasure to my lips, I felt myself unfurl for him. A tiny pod of life testing the earth for succor. As he adjusted and paced himself, driving deeper then easing away, I moved with him, encouraging him to take each second as he wanted. I didn't need tenderness. It was foreign to me. What I wanted was absolution. I wanted pain. If it meant I pushed him harder, driving him to greater frenzy, then I would give him that.

Because he deserved it, and so did I. The Nocturnes had shown me what life truly was. I was not fae. I was not human. I was not a daylighter.

I was Sidhe. And the Sidhe thrived in darkness and violence.

A tear might have pooled in the corner of my eye and dribbled down my temple. Guilt surged, threatening to overwhelm the sandbags I'd placed along the narrow river of memory. I thought of that boy and felt the banks give way.

My tears must have touched his skin, because he paused. His eyes bore into mine. I clawed at his back, urging him on, pushing him past the moment I didn't want to consider.

"Stop," he said.

I froze. Terrified I'd done something wrong.

He shook his head the way a dog might with water in its ears. "Not this way," he said and cupped both sides of my head with his hands and his thumbs smeared the tears on the crest of my cheek. "Not if it causes you pain. I'd rather break on rock than let you fly in pain."

No one had ever paused in the taking of their pleasure for my sake. No lover had read my pain like a sacred text and lingered over the ink seeping into the pages.

Something shifted, then. The armor I'd forged over my lifetime to mask the memory of that boy and my guilt weakened at the joints, widened to allow him in. I wasn't sure how I would withstand the quiet invasion of his compassion.

So I reached for him again, stroking his jawline. "It doesn't hurt."

His gaze softened. "I didn't mean physical pain, pretty bird."

I found it hard to meet his eyes with mine. My palm skimmed his back. I swallowed down all the memories threatening to overwhelm me.

"They are nothing," I said. "Echoes from a well long gone dry."

"But they're painful still," he said thoughtfully as he examined my face. Whatever he saw there caused him to roll onto his side and gather me onto his chest. With a tender urging of his palms, he helped me straddle his hips then planted his hands on my waist, down low where he could guide me further.

"Think of me," he said. "The boy is gone. He is a shadow now. What we weave here frees you from that guilt."

I nodded, not trusting my voice. For the first time in half a lifetime, I didn't feel as if I was drowning in darkness. The boy's shadow retreated into the ceiling like a tide peeling back from the shore, and I drew in a shuddering inhale as it went.

Sensing it, Stone moved again, slowly at first, letting me find the rhythm, then letting me take it.

"That's it," he murmured. "Good girl. You're doing so good. Take what you need. I'll be here when it's over."

Permission. It was a strange thing. I threw my head back, surrendering to him and taking him at once as I watched the shadows in the corners disappear. I thought I saw a small creature slipping back into the darkness along the wall. And then, that very darkness fractured into prisms of light as the crystal-studded ceiling winked back at me.

The iron bars I'd raised around myself, the darkness that I kept my greater self in, began to melt and meld together like smelted iron, glowing brighter. The feeling of lightness buoyed me, lifting me out of the forge. My heart soared as if it too had wings, stretching into the heavens he'd opened for me.

My release felt like those colors. It took my breath. Stole the next heartbeat, and left a single note thrumming deep in the marrow of my bones.

It vibrated until it became a single note, like the tapping of a finger on bare ivory. A note of language testing the air for another voice.

Heat shimmered between us. His breath hitched, and he looked at his wrist where bone jutted under the pressure of his grip; a gray vein unfurled in the shape of a single wing before it dimmed to black and finally disappeared.

Then, he hummed that same note now singing in my bones, and I knew he had marked me and I him. Not in flesh but in power, born of our natal magics now one. His magics hadn't recoiled at mine. After all I'd done, it accepted me.

When I realized I was floating again, wings reaching for the ceiling, he was right there with me, wrapped in my embrace and caught by my thighs. He reached up, fingertips brushing the star-shaped labradorite stone embedded at the apex, and looked into my face with all the wonder of a child.

For the first time in decades I felt no shame.

Later, we lay together on the fur. Candlelight played over his chest like a lover's touch. Sweat shimmered on his skin, making him look like carved marble and gold.

"Carraig," he said softly.

"What?" I asked, distracted by the way he looked.

"My true name." His broad, calloused, massive hands cupped the back of my nape. "You knew I could use yours against you, force a vow you would loathe. I could strip you bare of your power. Ruin your future and erase your past from the history of all Fae. And yet you gave it to me."

"I wanted you to see me," I whispered.

It was a risk, I knew, to be that honest. No one had trusted me with power unless it was to their benefit, expecting me to use it against an enemy or deliver death on a shadow's outline. That he would risk the same split something open inside me.

"Oh I see you, Ruvienne," he murmured. "You're the shadow that shapes itself into my greatest fear and desire. The perfume that I catch on an errant breeze. I've always seen you hiding in the dark, teasing me. And now that I recognize you, I want you to see me too."

The words struck cleaner than a blade and landed like a moth's kiss. I felt lightheaded. Giddy.

I rolled closer, draping my leg over his thigh, enjoying the warmth of his body against mine.

"Then I have your power now, too," I teased, the first hint of humor in centuries playing in the undertones of my voice. "I could destroy you with such knowledge."

For a heartbeat, I thought I'd gone too far, but then he brushed the hair back from my forehead. "I think you already have."

My heart squeezed at the comment. I'd never felt so utterly still. The predator in me was content to sit in the branches, eyes half-closed, glutted, warm. A feeling I'd not felt even in the days Enyali was alive. This was different. This was...completion.

"I will never use it," I said, the promise breaking free before I could think about the consequences . "From this moment to the last true beat of my heart, your true name will never pass my lips," I said, guiding his hand to my heart. "It lives here. Sacred. Safe."

He smiled and tapped my nose. "Not even if you face the Queen of the Darkness?"

"Not even then," I said. "Not even if you are called to take my life or I yours. I will never rob you of your power."

I traced the shell of his ear, marveling at its perfect shape. "Besides. Stone suits you."

He kissed my palm. A smile, true and unguarded, found me for the first time in centuries. Perhaps the first since Enyali's death, and I savored it because some part of me already knew: this moment, this warmth this peace—was the first and last time I would ever fee whole.

IN THE NOCTURNES, WHOLENESS never lasted. Peace was a temporary thing. In the quiet moments afterwards while he still lay splayed out, content, spent, I worried the bottom of my lip, waiting for the lightning to strike.

Oblivious to it, he rolled over to face me, his face golden in the firelight. His palm skimmed my arm thoughtfully.

"When I saw you at the stables, I wouldn't have guessed you had the power of flight."

"I don't," I said, relaxing beneath his touch, feeling as though I had been foolish to worry. "Only here, where the source is strongest. Where I'm authentically Sidhe."

"You are not fully Sidhe, then?" he said.

"Not fully alive," I corrected him. "I never was. It's why the Madre and the Morrakai insist on the Reavening."

He leaned back against the altar. "That's what you call the raids for males of power?"

"It's the whole of the rite. From the scrying of the seer, to the raids, to the casting of bones, to the...well, to what we just did." I bit my lip, my eyebrows scuttling down. "And for what happens next." I didn't want to mention the sacrifices that came after. I had put that behind me.

His sigh moved my hair, and I tucked it behind my ear as it crossed my forehead and caught in my eyelashes. I should cut it, I thought, looking at his bristle of hair. Shorter was better.

"We are neither of us what we thought, then," he mused aloud. I was so lost in my thoughts I didn't realize he'd spoken, and when I did, I was sure he hadn't meant to say it.

I pulled away, suspicion rising, coloring my voice. "What do you mean?"

He started, almost as though he didn't expect me to ask. Something moved over his expression, and my eyes narrowed.

"Something," I said.

I felt his shrug. "Just that I'm not fully fae," he said. "I thought you knew that."

The confession shocked me. "No." My stomach tightened, and a thought flitted through my mind that, perhaps knowing this, the Madre would not honor her promise. "If not fae, then what?"

"Oh, I have fae blood. Lots of it. But my mother was a human-fae hybrid. I have human blood in my veins."

"Impossible," I said. "You have magic."

He grinned. "Of course I have magic. My natals and innates are infused with a hefty amount of it, but there's power in humanity too."

I sucked the back of my teeth. "The humans have nothing but a penchant for clinging to life despite certain death."

He tapped my nose. "That's a sort of magic, is it not."

"It's ludicrous."

"You sound like my father. He feels like it's a stain on the bloodline. He couldn't imagine the magic of a mortal lust for life and blamed that strain of human blood in her death."

The rawness in his voice made him seem vulnerable, real, in a way the intimacy we'd just shared hadn't. I wanted to validate it, to show him I understood.

"You sound like you admire her."

He ran his hand through his hair. "Of course I did. She had a strength my father couldn't understand. The power of compassion, of forgiveness. They aren't exclusive to humanity, but the mortals understand it better than we do."

I remained silent as he dropped his hand to my hip. "Ilianna," he says. "Her true name, my mother. She bore three of us for a male who hated his love of her, thinking her humanity a weakness. Only two of us have her spark. My youngest brother the most."

I didn't need to ask which sibling that was. I'd seen him. A wisp of a high fae who seemed barely capable of holding himself together, as though the magic inside him was trying to tear him apart. It made sense that he had some of the frailty of humanity.

"My father sent me to her," he said in a soft voice. "To Aiofe. He wanted me to see if the queen was holding her enthralled."

I stiffened, because I knew exactly what that had to mean for a high fae to enter Kumara, a place of half-life and shadows.

"Did he kill you?" I asked softly and tried to add up how many years he might have wasted there, gaining power until his freedom from her clutches.

A short bark of humorless laughter. "Not quite. He was smarter than that. He drained me with his own teeth, just enough to make me start to waste before he had Blade heal me again."

That moment was the first time I'd heard true bitterness in his voice. It drew my hand to his throat, where I imagined his father had bitten him, wanting to add my own sort of healing to the wound there, and found instead the scar I'd left. I couldn't help stroking it, trying to make it disappear with my fingers.

His reaction was to hook my ankle with his, and my violence retreated in the face of the image of him being forced to stand in Aiofe's throne room, demanding answers of a queen who answered to no one.

"Was she?" I asked in a small voice.

His eyebrows inched up in query. "Was my mother being held in Kumara?" he asked. A shake of his head.

"No. Her humanity, that small spark allowed her to pass into another lifetime in the mortal world instead of ending her fae one."

I sucked in a breath at the magnitude of such a concept. "That's possible? How do you know?"

At that, he reached for my hand and pulled it to his chest, holding it there. Only after he spoke did I realize he was doing it to trap my hands from striking out.

"Aiofe let me see her," he said. "I watched her gathering herbs from her garden, using them to cast magics of protection over her new family, completely unaware of the one she'd left behind."

The emotion in his voice made my throat hurt, but I knew this wasn't the reason he still held my hands caged against his chest.

"What did that vision cost you?" I asked, feeling my heart start to hammer as my mind wandered over what Aiofe would demand for such a gift.

He rolled onto his side to face me, still holding my hand. Something in his expression sent a shiver up my spine.

"She didn't need to bargain with me, Ruby," he said. "She was like a mother to me when my own passed away. My father let her keep her suites in his mansion until she was sure Blade no longer needed her. She asked a boon of me and I agreed."

Even though I'd never shared Enyali's gift of prescience, I started to tremble.

"But why?" I asked. "Why would she do that?"

He shrugged. "What do most fae do things for if not for love? She desires vengeance. I didn't ask of whom or why. She said all I needed to do was make sure the moment I realized I was being tracked by someone that I was never alone. That I should ensure I kept about me fae I trusted and who would kill for me."

"But Aiofe does not have the gift of prescience. She's the daughter of an underworld titan. She knows only darkness, not light. Those powers are light magic."

He tightened his grip. "She has a thrall with the gift, though, doesn't she?"

My mouth went dry. It took a few moments to realize what he was telling me. A confession. A secret that I'd not even guessed at when this all began.

That Aiofe had used Enyali's gift to set her plan—whatever it was—into motion.

"She wasn't after your magic at all," I said in a strangled voice.

When I tried to pull away, he wrestled me close again. I didn't want to look him in the face. He knew. He knew about Enyali and the vow all this time, and he let me think this was all my fault.

The betrayal was like swallowing shards of glass.

More than that, I felt foolish. He'd told me clearly enough before that he knew Aiofe. How had I been stupid enough to believe she would want him dead?

I was still reeling from the information when he spoke again, tearing my attention back to him.

"Your sister knew," he whispered. "She knew all this and she accepted it. That's why she died. Not because you did anything to get her killed. She chose it."

I pulled away this time, using the leverage of my feet against his shins. "No," I said. "She would never have chosen death."

Freedom came swiftly. Too swiftly. And only because he relented beneath a barrage of kicks that were terribly unsatisfying to deliver.

He got to his knees as I scrambled to my feet. "It's true, Ruby," he said. "Aiofe told me. She said Enyali tempted that angel not so she could bring him to the Nocturnes for the Reavening. She wasn't interested in birthing another seer."

My chest felt like ice was forming. "You're lying."

His face softened as he held out his hands to me. "You know that's impossible."

I looked at his outstretched palms and slapped them away. "Why would she do that? Why would she court death and let the Madre—let me—think it was because she wanted to extend the seer line?"

"Think about it," he said. "She knew the angel had more power than she did. She courted him knowing he would kill her and she would go to the queen. Damn the seers of this world, for they know things so complex even the beat of a butterfly's wing carries no mystery."

My head was shaking so hard, my neck hurt. "She wouldn't do that. She wouldn't leave me." I hated how high-pitched my voice had grown.

"Why would she do that?" My voice finally broke, and he stood to gather me in his arms. I pushed him away.

His hands fell to his sides, but they fidgeted there as though he was struggling not to grab for me.

"I don't know," he said. "I doubt even Aiofe does. But I do know your sister knows. And I believe she thinks you do too."

"Fuck you," I said. "You don't know her. You don't know me." I scalded him with a glare. "I don't even know you anymore."

"I'm the same fae who held you a moment ago," he breathed. "I'm the same fae who let you bring me here. While that's no accident, I didn't expect to feel for you. Aiofe left out that part."

"More lies."

He sighed. "Would your sister lie?"

I considered telling him to go to hell with his questions, but a stab of pain shot through my stomach. I doubled over so suddenly I almost passed out.

He was next to me in an instant, holding my hand and bracing me against his shoulder. "What is it? What's wrong?"

I swatted at him, trying to push him away but another slice of pain razored through my stomach and shot up to my throat. A shudder moved through me.

He didn't hesitate a moment longer. I was in his arms before the next pain stabbed my insides. "Ruby?" he said, his voice frantic as he carried me back to the furs that lay in front of the altar. "What is it? What's wrong?"

I'd never known what happened in the huts and roundhouses where the others went after the casting. When the sisters took their prized males to their beds and coupled under the spells of the Madre. I only knew that hours later, they either held infant females in swaddling cloths or they were found dead inside their huts.

Those who died giving birth to stillborn infants were burned along with every male who had been raided for.

And I knew in that instant why I was in pain.

"The quickening has begun," I said, panting through the pain.

"What does that mean?"

He clutched my hand tighter now. Some small part of me warmed at the thought his fear was for me and not what it might mean for him. And that made the difference. I forgot the anger of betrayal. There was only him and me and a child within that stretched already at the strictures of its boundaries.

I sucked in enough breath to bear through the next jolt of agony. "It means the babe is growing."

"Babe?" he asked. "Are you telling me we have made a child together?"

"It's why you're here, is it not?" I almost laughed at his expression of confusion and wonder, but another stab shot through me, stealing my breath. "Sevina's magic ensured it."

"How long?" he asked as he laid his palm on my stomach.

I shook my head. "I don't know." I panted, sucked in a breath, cried out because I couldn't cage the sound.

He looked terrified. "I don't know what to do."

"Just talk to me," I said, trying not to break down. It hurt so much. Like sharp points of glass slicing through each organ. "Listening to your voice helps." I gripped his hand in mine and squeezed as I panted through the pain.

He did talk to me then, in a hushed, calm voice. He spoke of his mother and the dream she had for her sons to be part of something important. He told me about his youngest brother, a young fae with so much power it overwhelmed him and sent him to a wasting bed repeatedly.

He spoke of his half-brother, and how he believed there was something inside him that might rival the shadows of the Nocturnes and his worry that his brother might succumb to that darkness.

His worries, his hopes and dreams. All of this and more he rambled on about, doing his best to soothe me. It worked most of the time, but when the worst of the pains came, pulling me into an instinctive bow out of sheer agony, he remained calm even though his voice trembled when he spoke.

It was he who noticed my belly growing. I was too lost in holding onto my sanity in the whirl of emotion and pain. He planted his palm on the swell of it and looked into my face.

"A child," he said in wonder. "A fae child."

A rarity indeed. "Not fae," I said, correcting him. "Sidhe. She will be brought up here. She will be taught the ways of the Nocturnes."

His mouth twisted in realization. "And she will murder fae males and become a brood mare for your Madre."

"Not just for Sevina," I gasped out as another spasm wrung out my stomach. "For the whole of the Nocturnes. She will bring the magic of your lineage to the weave of ours. We may have a seer finally if all goes well."

I tried to smile, but it felt more like a grimace. The words tasted sour. For some reason, the victory of knowing I'd succeeded, that I'd managed to win his escape from the fate every male suffered here at the cost of my child's, felt wrong.

I felt for my stomach and touched his fingers. He flipped his hand over to grasp mine and then laid it flat along the curve of my belly.

"She shouldn't live in darkness," he whispered. "She is of the light."

At his words, a driving pang cut through my womb and twisted. A sharp hiss escaped me, such that I couldn't find the energy or the breath to argue. Both of his hands cupped the growing swell of my stomach as I leaned back, planting my hands behind me. My breath came in short, ragged gusts.

"It's getting bigger," he said. "I feel it kicking."

"Her," I gasped out. "I feel her moving."

It wasn't a lie, but it wasn't the truth, either. I knew he meant the babe inside was a wonder of movement, but for me, it was an agony. With each inch she grew, each time she stretched and kicked and tested the boundaries, I could feel her growing more impatient and restless. She was angry at the confinement. She raged against it.

Feeling her move was like being clawed by long, heated talons. Every inch of my body dripped with sweat. My stomach bulged and came to an agonizing point, and I knew the feel of her nails scraping at the inside of my flesh, trying to dig herself out.

"Sidhe," I ground out through gritted teeth at the sensation, disappointment flooding me. "She is meant for the darkness after all."

He stroked my stomach. "No," he said. "No. No. No. She is high fae. She can't be confined to this awful place where she will learn that males are expendable donors to be consumed or burned or gods know what else you do to them."

His expression took on a sort of panic the first time I saw any such emotion on his face. A different sort of pang went through me then.

It wasn't because of the words he spoke of the homeland I'd known and been exiled from. I had my own conflicts over the realm that bore me. No. It was the pain I heard in his voice at the thought that he would have to abandon his child here to a place that was more violent than any Shadow Court.

It was the knowledge that I couldn't change the future. I'd made a vow. For his life, I'd taken the bone vow. It wasn't something that could be broken.

"She is part of the bargain, Stone," I whispered, afraid she would hear. "Your life depends on her existence here in the darkness. I vowed it with the bones that knit me. My womb remembers it."

It hurt to see the look on his face. Defeat. That's what it was. I'd long forgotten the meaning of emotion, burying every telltale sign of it in as dark a place as the Nocturnes. Self-preservation, I'd told myself. Denying the signs of emotion made it easier for me to pretend it didn't exist, and if emotion didn't exist then I could do the hard things to stay alive.

But I read the defeat on his face. The sadness. The regret. And I wanted more than anything to make it better.

"I know the power of a vow, Ruby," he said. "But this one... this one isn't right."

"What would you have me do?" I asked in a whisper. "It is done."

"Take my life," he said, his hand full on the curve of my belly. It had gone quiet in the last moments, as though she was listening. "Buy hers with mine."

The words gutted me. How could I bear losing him after all this. The Madre. The Morrakia. Nothing mattered. This was all for him.

Panic clawed at my throat at his words. I shook my head, peeling his hand away from the swell of the growing thing inside me.

"I will not," I said and struggled to crab walk away from him. I gained an inch or so before his hands clamped down on my ankles, holding me fast.

"Tell your madre I will service the Morrakai. All of them." He sounded desperate. "I'll even take on the old shriveled bitch herself, surrender to the blade when it's done—"

"Not just by blade," I interjected, a sort of hatefulness in my voice. "They may cut you, they may burn you, skin you, or even consume you. Your bones will be ground to dust and used to fertilize the herb garden. Is that what you want, Stone? For a child you've never met? An infant fae who might be male and murdered the moment it's born."

"You said it was a she," he argued.

I dropped my gaze, and his fingers climbed my calf as he shimmied toward me.

"You made the vow when she meant nothing to you or me," he said, his voice frantic. "She was an idea, a concept. Something not yet pulled from the ether. I know why you made the vow. I understand it. But she is none of those things now. She is here. She is part of us."

Another pain shot through me, this time strong enough to pull a loud groan from me. A loud clicking and clacking began outside the temple, the sisters sensing the imminent birth. Their excitement carried through the crystals and down into the sanctuary. They tinkled and shook with their piercing chatter.

Sevina's magic crept in through the center hole in the temple's arched ceiling. It wafted down with the lightness of a wisp of smoke and coiled in the air, testing. I almost felt it inhale.

"It's time," I said, and he swallowed. "She's coming, Stone. I need you to leave. Now. While you can."

He shook his head.

"You have to. Things can get...difficult when a babe is born here. The Morrakai, they get frenzied. It has been a long time since the realm has seen a seer. They will not be able to control themselves."

"I'm not leaving." He gripped my hand tighter as another spasm curled my toes and hollowed me out.

"She will have wings, I think," I murmured and found it strange that the words were so wispy, like the smoke of Sevina's magic.

"Ruby?" he said, urgency painting his voice. "Something's wrong."

It took a huge effort to turn my head in his direction. His face blurred out of focus for a moment then sharpened. I blinked, and it seemed to take forever. The cramps, the sharp pains were easing. I felt flooded with warmth. Everything below my waist felt covered in slick oil.

I thought I heard him curse, but I couldn't be sure. Everything seemed like it was suddenly coming through ears wadded with cotton. The darkness started creeping into the corners again.

Then there was excruciating agony all through my body. My back arched back in a spasm so sharp and hard that my head slammed against the flagstones. The moment of respite was brief, and it was over.

I was fully aware now, and fully aware that something was indeed wrong.

"She's not coming the right way," I yelled, and yet it came out as a harsh whisper. "She's not—"

"I know," he said, scrambling to move between my thighs, hoisting my knees up and over his shoulders. "What the fuck," he growled. "Does no one help? Do they leave you here to live or die?" His face between my knees was so pale it glowed in the dark. "Fuck, Ruby. What do I do? She's tearing you to pieces."

Chapter 18

EVERY SECOND TURNED TO agony after that. I knew nothing but sweat and panting and living by seconds of sheer, gasping pain that felt like thousands of razors stinging over my skin and sharp knives stabbing my belly.

We labored together, Stone and I. Over the next gods knew how many moments or hours. Alone in the weaving candlelight with me biting back shrieks of pain and him coaxing and coaching and growling that he wasn't ready for this. He had no healing powers.

By the time I felt myself tear by inches and warmed by a rush of blood, I knew our labors were for nothing.

"Your mother's name?" I breathed out. "Tell me your mother's name again."

He looked up at me, his face no longer calm and powerful but pinched by regret and fear. I fell back against the altar, letting my legs sag with the brief respite of a contraction ending.

Afraid as he looked, he marshaled his expression and answered me without question.

"Ilianna," he said.

I nodded, my hand feeling for the slickness between my legs. So much blood there, and all for nothing. I couldn't feel her hair or her head in the warmth of my core.

"That's her name," I said. "If she lives. That's her true name."

He shook his head, tears leaking from his eyes. "She'll live," he said. "And so will you."

I tried to laugh and cough instead. "The Nocturnes takes its vows seriously," I said. "It digs its claws into its daughters. It's not going to let me free, and that's ok. I've made my peace with that. I'll see Enyali again." I tried a feeble smile and managed it.

To his credit, he didn't argue. Rather, he held my hand again as another wave of pain took me. For a moment, I lost the feel of his fingers as I slid into another realm. I saw Enyali there, a shadow with a tremor of a smile, beckoning me.

Then I returned to the sanctuary with a slam. Footsteps rustled over stone. Shadows gathered. Whispers of familiar voices fingered their way through my consciousness.

I blinked to see a cluster of sisters standing in a tight circle around us. Shadows sliced over the wall in urgent movements as Stone argued with the Madre, shouting at her that she should do something or lose both assets. I guessed those assets were me and the babe.

Someone shrieked. A high-pitched banshee sound that made the crystals in the ceiling cry out. I didn't realize it was me until a soft, wet sluicing moved through me and slid between my thighs, and the screaming immediately stopped.

The chamber went entirely silent.

I didn't dare breathe. The edges of my vision were so dark I couldn't make out Stone's head until he stroked my face and drew my attention to where he was sitting beside me.

"She's out," he said. "She's safe."

Safe. And yet something in his voice, something in the eerie silence of the room, told me there was heavier, less positive news. I didn't need to hear what it was to know.

I was dying.

Sevina lifted the babe from between my legs, holding her up for me to see. Slick with blood and glistening with fluids, my daughter looked pink and fat with two legs, two arms, and all the requisite toes and fingers.

"No wings," I said, and Stone brushed my hair back.

"She's perfect."

But Ilianna wasn't crying. Wasn't breathing. Wasn't moving. The moment was a vacuum that made me think I'd gone deaf until Sevina spoke, crashing into the awful silence with hateful words.

"She's human," she said with disgust. "We bargained for a natal magic that is mortal in nature." She cast Stone a look of rage. "All this for nothing."

He grinned as he held her gaze. "Then you'll have no need of her," he said, holding out his arms. "So I'll thank you to give me my daughter."

Sevina's eyes narrowed. "You think to take this magicless creature from us, Stone of Terran?" She sucked the back of her teeth. "It is near death and dying. Whatever magic she has will feed the sisters." A quick, scanning examination with a hateful eye. "She isn't much but she will roast just fine."

Stone's roar at Sevina's words was enough to deafen the entire host of Morrakai. The way he moved, storming to his feet to launch himself at Sevina, was terrifying enough to make a stalwart soldier gasp in fear.

But he wasn't fast enough to wrest the babe from Sevina's grasp as she held the infant by the ankle, dangling her over my stomach as she inspected her in the candlelight as if she were a rat found pilfering the food stores.

In truth, no one could be fast enough. Not compared to the mother who bore the endangered child.

By some miracle, I found the energy to wrest the babe from the Madre's grip. She was slippery and she was cold but my hands were sure, despite the trembling. I scrambled back against the altar, letting my shoulders rest there, defended from the rear as I cradled the tiny thing against my chest.

Stone was still scuffling with the host of Morrakai. Sevina stood with her bloodied hands tucked over her crossed arms. A hush fell over the room, even though I knew the sounds of battle should be loud and obnoxious.

Magic, I knew. Nocturnal magic wrapped shadows around me. The last vestige of my power coming to claim me.

I looked down at the tiny miracle, and something inside me split like tectonic plates shrugging each other off. The chasm filled with tears and emotion.

Mine. This mostly human creature was mine, borne of a beloved bond that I knew I was going to have to break.

My existence in this realm would end soon. The darkness would ferry me to Kumara. But I would not be a whisper in the shadows, falling silent in a hush. I would be a serpent banked in the embers of a fire they'd thought long dead, striking back when everyone thought my venom long burned away.

A half-smile curved my lips as I thought of it. Stone's words. Stone's own warcraft. It gave me pleasure to think he'd taught me something.

I watched him as he fought the grip the Morrakai had on his arms when they pulled them back behind him. A fresh cut on his cheek below his left eye bloomed with bruising beneath his skin. His chest was heaving.

Even though the shadows gathered closer, I could still see his face, his posture, the way his shoulders, though pinned so far upward on his frame that sweat was breaking out on his forehead. His lips pulled back to bare his teeth. He'd lost all the bargaining chips he'd come with. All except for me.

Except it was too late for me. And it was too late for the babe. I stole a glance down at her face. She had all the strength of him in her features. Humanity shone through her skin, all but obliterating the faint shimmer of fae.

I sent out tendrils of magic, sniffing her solar plexus for evidence of it, and a thready tendril of energy hummed back at me, barely discernible.

A bargain was a bargain. The Madre had made one with me in blood and bone, and I would force her to honor it before it broke of its own accord and she could lay claim to him.

"Your vow, Sevina," I said in a level voice. "You have to let him go. You swore it."

She hissed back at me, enraged that I would dare remind her. Especially now. Especially when my death was so close. But she nodded, and the Morrakai curled their lips at me.

When Stone broke free of their slackened hold, he surged toward where I lay cradling our daughter against the altar, a red tide flooding his cheeks and forehead. He spun, back toward me, with barely a glance down and spread his hands out at his sides, palms aimed at Sevina and the Morrakai.

"I'm not leaving without our daughter." He pulled a flame of magic into his palms. His first show of magic in the Nocturnes. For the babe. For me. "And I'm not leaving without you."

I knew he meant his words. He meant it all. He wouldn't leave. Not until he'd done all he could to pull us all out of the Nocturnes. But he would die here if he waited. And so would she.

My heart squeezed at the truth of it, something I'd needed all these years. Acceptance. Love. The chance of being seen as worthy to someone. And here it was. That aching, painful gift given without a single hesitation. It was all there in the curve of his nape, the bristle of hair. I brought to mind every feature I couldn't now see on his face, and I savored it for one more moment.

And then, I did what I had to because I couldn't let him stay. I couldn't let him die here.

"Go," I said to him, drawing a look back over his shoulder. The confusion that suffused his features was a sharp pain in my stomach. "Go now."

"I can't. I won't."

I forced my mouth to form a dry, taunting grin as I memorized every beloved feature, as the Morrakai smirked behind him, as I pulled to me every last ounce of energy I had to weave the lie I knew I had to speak. Convincing. Masking the falsehood with truth so he would believe it.

"Oh, Stone," I said. "You don't understand, do you? I used your humanity." I smiled, though I knew it wafted over my face like mist and disappeared again. It was so difficult to hold shape.

"You were a useful tool," I said, the strain of effort making my voice gritty. "You and your secret magic of humanity have robbed the Nocturnes of this child and freed me from it as well. If not for that human weakness in you, none of this would be possible."

I purposefully used his father's words to taunt him, and I knew the effect it would have on him. Even knowing it was intentional, it still hurt to see his face turn ugly.

Hurt rode his features like a rabid beast. "Your Madre was right," he said in a strangled voice. "You are a mercenary to the core."

"Leave now," I said, urgency painting my voice as I sensed the last light leaving the babe. I know he felt it too, because his gaze flickered to our daughter's face and his brow scuttled down.

"Leave," I said again. "While the Morrakai and the Madre are still bound by the bargain. "Save yourself at least, you fool. The babe is the Nocturne's and you will be too if you linger one more moment."

I inclined my head, doing my best to make it look smug and not bowed by the weight of shame and grief. Beneath shuttered lids, I watched the way his shoulders slumped.

He might have remained had the Madre not turned a smug look in his direction. She held up her hand, staying the Morrakai's grip on him.

As they released him, she laughed. "We may yet have our turns, sisters," she said, gesturing at me. "See how she struggles to hold her form. The vow may break before he escapes."

It was true. Even as she spoke, a shudder of pain passed over me, turning tissue to shadow. The unmistakable feeling of release as one by one the feathers from my wings let go their tenuous hold of my tissues. The cloak of darkness swallowed the chamber bit by bit.

"Go now," I croaked out. "You're nothing here, Stone of Terran, but a means to an end, and you couldn't even provide that. Your human magic is a waste. It's a curse."

I lifted our daughter in my arms to show him her paling face.

"This creature your magics foisted upon us? It's worthless. You are worthless. Reclaim your shame and save your body before the Morrakai end you and you travel to Kumara with me. The next time I see you, I'll bear a message from your daughter and you can know she is here, and you'll know your weakness is the reason for it."

Those last words were difficult. I heard a tinge of regret in my voice and feared he'd hear it too. But mercifully, his lips curled back, showing teeth that seemed more canine than man. He might have shifter magic in him too, but I knew I'd never see it. What I did see clearly was the hatred in his eyes. The loathing shuddered through him so viscerally it shook his hands and bowed his head.

A swallow moved through his throat before he directed that same hateful look to each of the Morrakai, landing finally on the Madre.

"You will all feel the wrath of this moment," he said in a bitter voice. "Someday. I will end you all."

She blinked at him and gestured toward Askrid. "Enjoy your journey," she said to Stone. "There is no safe way out of the Nocturnes save the magic that brought you here or death. And only one of those things is possible now."

She grinned.

His head bobbed as he chuckled. With a side-step, he put himself in reach of the cranny where my casting bone had rested. His hand burrowed inside and came out with a coin.

He held it high. "You think I'd bargain with the hell-hound and not carry a failsafe from her kingdom?"

He clutched it tightly as he glanced my way. "Goodbye, Ruby Morvannon."

With that, he whispered a few words of the old language and with a laugh that evaporated as he did, found his way out of the Nocturnes on the wings of magic as old as Kumara itself. I was certain I saw a snake's eye in the lingering ashes of the scrying bowl.

Even as he evaporated, another thing phased into the place he left. It looked like him, this thing, but it lay writhing on the floor of the sanctuary as if in pain. Trying to find its legs, trying to gain full form, its hunger a pang of energy that coiled throughout the chamber.

"A ferryman," said Askrid in calm disgust as she watched it take shape. A full heartbeat pulsed before the entire caste of Morrakai shrieked and clicked and clacked their rage.

Then they descended upon it.

In seconds, they had torn the newborn demon to pieces. Its blood coated the altar and filled the scrying bowl, dampening the last remains of the embers within.

But as they executed the horror Stone had brought into the Nocturnes, I watched the shadows where he disappeared. Though I knew the rest could not see him as he fled, I held onto every minuscule atom of his form until he was completely gone.

With a shuddering sigh, I dropped my head back against the altar. There was nothing left of the wings I'd been so proud of. The feathers had left a bedding beside me in iridescent colors. Each fall of every one hurt, but losing him hollowed me out completely.

I lifted my gaze to the crystals above me as the Morrakai consumed the newborn demon in revoltingly loud noises.

After a moment, I felt the Madre standing over me and shifted my gaze, no longer able to do more than tighten my embrace around my daughter.

"You're wasting, Ruby," she said. "You may as well leave the child. We'll feast on her flesh and consume whatever latent magic she holds."

I shook my head. "No. You won't have her." Ilianna wasn't all human. There was a tiny bit of fae inside, and I wasn't about to let go of her. "She's mine."

I held her even tighter, pulling to mind the feel of Stone's body the moment I'd pulled him against me when I'd decided to drag him to the Nocturnes with me, drawing out the memory of how his body fit against me and inside me when we'd joined together.

The memory of his warmth on my skin remained until I let the last bit of shadow claim me. And when it came for me, I surrendered with a smile on my face.

Because the Nocturnes would not get our child. Not while there was magic in her still.

"She's coming with me," I said, my voice nothing more than a ragged whisper. "She's coming to Kumara."

Chapter 19

Ilianna died in Kumara. At least, the fae part of her did. I felt the last of her magic waste as I slipped into the queen's throne room like a wet and shivering newborn.

My breath caught in the back of my throat as it left her and collected in the corners. I watched her fae magic shimmer there for a moment, wonder making my chest feel like it was floating too.

"She's human now," said a voice from behind me, startling me. "What's left of her."

I swung around, cradling the chilling body against my breast.

"She is," I told Aiofe. "You have no hold over her here."

The queen lowered her head, eyes shuttered. "You think you're more clever than the queen who is the darkness? Bringing a half-breed fae into my throne room so she can shed her fae-ness?"

"I think I'm desperate," I said and held Ilianna out.

She looked at my daughter dispassionately. "Your sister told me this would happen. She told me Terran's son would fall in love with you. She said you would birth a child of human magic." She snorted, as if she'd only just begun to think it could be true, when all along she'd thought it fancy.

She stepped closer, and I pulled the child back against my breast, feeling the warmth leave her. She still hadn't cried. Still hadn't made a single mewling sound, and I thrust my chin up.

"She's strong," I said. "Resilient as I am. She can survive in the mortal realm."

Aiofe's mouth twitched. "Your sister told me the same thing," she said, and then her voice grew discordant and swelling the way Enyali's always got when she forecast something of magnitude. "She will live a long and powerful life and she will know nothing of her parents, and yet she will not be free of the Nocturnes. The reavening is in her the way her blood carries iron. She will continue the practice in her world."

"What will I care?" I asked. "She will live. That's all that matters. The men of the human race and what happens to them is no concern of mine."

"And Stone?" she asked.

"He doesn't need to know his daughter lives," I said, shrugging.

"He hates you."

I nodded, and while the truth hurt, it felt good too. Like rubbing a knot of pain from a shoulder. "He does."

She cast a long look at Ilianna. We both knew the only way a human could enter Kumara was if there was fae blood or a fae bond. Ilianna had both, but with the fae magic gone, she could not remain in the queen's grasp for long. The realms would right themselves. A fae changeling might return as the babe took its place in the world, but that would be all.

"She will need nurturing in the human world," Aiofe mused aloud. 'You're too wasted already to be that mother."

The shadows quickened with noise. The bars that held the worst of the thralls rose from the darkness like a white pebble being lifted from a dark well. But I paid no mind. It was the queen's way of gathering magic. Nothing could hurt me here now. And yet, what came to shape from within the shadows made me gasp.

Enyali. She came as if on a breeze, collecting shape like leaves gathering on the ground and swirling upward in air currents.

Tears gathered on my cheeks. "Sister," I said. "I have brought you a niece."

"And not a moment too soon," Enyali said in those sweet notes I remembered, putting an ache in my heart.

I held the infant out so she could see. "She's perfect," I said, thinking of Stone's words. "Perfectly human."

Her mouth twisted wryly but not unkindly. "So she will leave this place and become part of the mortal realm. Pity in some ways. Her fate will accompany the rise and fall of twin gods who will use the earthen realm for a playground."

She inclined her head thoughtfully. "But you have done well, sister. What you have wrought in darkness will bring light to them in some distant future, but here and now, I feel the pain that beat of a butterfly's wing has caused."

Aiofe inched closer as Enyali spoke as though she thought me too distracted by my sister's voice to notice. But I did. And I pulled back, afraid she might harm Ilianna.

Her glance upward suggested she'd not expected my reaction. Even she could not wholly mask her interest in a mortal thing entering the Stygian Darkness.

"Humans are a morbid curiosity at best," she said. "Yet this one seems to possess an interesting destiny." She canted her head the other way, in the manner of dogs sussing out some strange new creature. "Curious."

When she turned to Enyali, all interest had abandoned her features, and it had returned to that stoic mask. "You, of course, already know your destiny."

Enyali inclined her head. "You are releasing me, finally."

My heart soared. Both of them free. It was more than I could have dreamed.

Enyali reached for the babe and I offered her.

"Her name is Ilianna," I said, giddy with joy and sadness over the things I'd both won and lost. Still, I focused on the fact that the babe would live. Stone might never know the truth, but it helped to know that at least they would both live.

Even if I couldn't enjoy life with my mate, it was worth everything I'd done, every cloaked truth I'd told. My sister took the infant from me and kissed her lightly on the forehead.

"I'll keep her safe," she said as she backed away into the shadows. The air hissed with power. Aiofe was already letting go, and the child was already reclaiming the right of her humanity. She didn't belong here and the earthen realm was taking her back. Would she be whole in that realm? Would she breathe and have a heartbeat? I had risked much in the hope that she would, and the urge to know for sure that risk had paid off drew me toward the shadows with them.

Aiofe's gentle hand on my arm held me back. "Not you, Morvannon," she said, guiding me away from the shadows where Enyali was already glowing brighter in the darkness and the babe in her arms already gone.

"You'll see him again," Enyali whispered. "Tell him your daughter says hello. Let him believe she still lives."

I shot a harried glance toward Enyali as I resisted.

"The darkness is claiming them," I said. "They are already journeying on the light to the mortal realm. I need to go now."

Aiofe shook her head. "This is your realm now," she said, directing my gaze once more to the shadows, where Enyali too had disappeared, and then to my own body, weak and ravaged. Wasted and unable to thrive beyond Kumara's threshold for decades to come perhaps.

"You belong here with me," she said. "Your daughter will be safe. She will not be bound to the Nocturnes as you were. And your sister, too, is free of them. She earned the powers I gave to her. I regret nothing."

"You gave my sister more magic?"

She nodded. "She served me well here in Kumara. She earned her release and more. But you, Morvannon, you have more to do. As your sister foretold, you and I are joined in this destiny. One that will liberate an entire fae realm some day when you regain enough power to ascend from the Nocturnes as she has, and as much as it pains me to hold you here, it must be done."

My stomach roiled into knots. Enyali's predictions always came true.

"You speak of my death," I said carefully, testing the meaning of her words. "And yet I am here, wasting."

Aiofe smiled wanly, showing a hint of teeth, suggesting she was caging some secret behind her canines.

"Your sister sees your energy on a dark wind, brushing brambles aside from a dark cave as it rises to the heavens and dissipates to open air far too many years from now to touch your daughter's face. She will be gone by then, in the way of mortals, but your seer has told me that some day your magics will join with Stone's." She tapped her chin thoughtfully. "Although I would like to think she's wrong. I always liked the boy and would hope for his very long *fae* life."

She stressed the word fae in a strange manner, and a pang went through me, not of regret, but of joy. Stone would live. My daughter would live. A dozen lifetimes in Kumara would be apt payment for such a bargain if that's what it took. And if I was fortunate enough to find Stone's magic on an errant breeze someday, each moment I spent in the darkness would be worth it.

My eyes eased themselves closed, imagining that moment. It was far away, but still I could sense it. A lifetime. Perhaps more. It didn't matter the time, didn't matter how many generations. I would wait an eternity.

"Until then, I suppose, I must wait."

She sighed heavily. "As must I for my own vengeance."

Bending to unlace her boots as though they were hurting her feet, she released an irritable groan. Perhaps she just wanted rid of the trappings of fae and wanted to slip back into her pure form.

She discarded them to a corner and arched backward, cracking her spine audibly, and as I watched the fae form slid from her body with a mere shiver, allowing the hellhound to climb her from the feet upward. It stopped just short of her torso, turning her beauty into a misshapen half-fae half hound creature that looked somehow more terrifying than either could be alone. It was only when she gestured to the shadows that I understood she had more to say before she surrendered to her true self.

I waited, breath caught in my throat.

"You will not simply waste here, gathering your magic from my source," she said after a time. "You are a mercenary. You will earn your magic back."

Something in her voice shot a tingle down my spine at her words, as audible as a soft hiss, the way a cobra might warn an intruder that it was getting too close.

"I don't understand," I said.

"Don't you?" she asked lightly. "The Nocturnes have enjoyed isolation too long without seeding me their power."

A jolt of power bullied its way through my skin. It burned in my palms, seared spots on my back where my wings would be. When they pierced my skin, falling free and spreading out, it was painful enough to bring me to my knees.

The queen looked me over, a smirk seaming her lips. "This is one thing your sister did not foresee," she said, the grin widening until her teeth caught on her lips. "That the darkness does not reveal its secrets any more than damp, black earth surrenders to the wind. I am The Darkness. And I have no fate that can be scryed from the depths of some watery bowl."

She stretched one arm elegantly upward, watching as the high fae curves gave way to the muscled sinews of hellhound form. "Your sister served me well, and while I don't forget such loyalty, my magic is never free."

At her words, my lungs inhaled on their own, shooting energy to my limbs, making my knees tremble, then lock. Somehow, impossibly, the queen was granting me magic. Enough to gain strength again, a power not borrowed from the Nocturnes but tethered instead to Aiofe herself.

"A life for a life," she said. "Power for power."

"I'm not afraid to die," I said, my eyes narrowing. If she wanted the last dregs of my magic, she could have it.

"Death is not yours, here, Morvannon," she said. "But another's is. I want you to collect it for me."

"Sevina," I guessed.

Her chin thrust upward in answer as it surrendered to the transformation creeping up her body. I knew she could shift in a heartbeat, but she slowed it, forcing me to witness every inch of torturous alteration, a demonstration of her dominion and control.

I've never refused a kill. Not for mercy. Not for guilt or love. Not demi-gods, vampires, or fae. I don't quibble over the lives I take. I give a good, clean kill with no loose ends.

And because of that, for the magic she poured into me, for the sister she'd liberated, the daughter she'd saved, I would give her this thing she demanded. I would serve the Queen of Darkness in her Kumara, honing my power until the day I rose again to earn my true death.

Because Enyali was never wrong. Stone and I were mates. Fated. Bound. Inevitable. And even if it was as only as the wind that lifted a falcon to the heavens, I would find my way back to him.

Epilogue

ENYALI, THE LAST OF the Nocturne seers, forged her way through woods and bracken, the weight of her sister's newborn bundled tightly to her chest.

The visions had driven her here to the mortal realm, out of Kumara and into daylight, because this child needed the mortal world now, not shadow. The fate that sprawled out ahead of her was one of power, and in realms steeped in magic, she would be helpless.

The infant's warmth, tucked into furs Aiofe had provided so the child could cling to her tenuous heat, warmed Enyali's skin. So too did the unfamiliar sun shredding the forest with light. The blazing sun might have blinded her once, in the days when she dwelled in shadows. Now, even after living a lifetime within the heart of darkness, she welcomed its burn on her skin. It took several hours before she could split open her eyelids enough to watch the terrain, feeling her way at first with echolocation, and then—when the woods gave way to grassy fields—with her toes and elbows and ears.

The hum of renewed magic pulsed through her body with ever-growing intensity. One thing was certain and unexpected: Aiofe's magic was strong. It heightened Enyali's already potent prescience to levels she had never thought possible, but it also stretched that power out behind her like breadcrumbs from a blackened path.

If she felt for those crumbs, she could almost see the trail they left behind her to the shadowy entrance of Kumara. If she scanned the horizon, she sensed them peppering paths ahead, splitting into dozens of trails that evaporated into the distance of the future. So many pathways, so many voices—a smothering weight on her shoulders, a cacophony in her ears.

In some visions she delved into the depths of Aiofe's memories and into Aiofe's future—the one tangled with the Shadow Court's fall and Stone's bloodline. There she saw betrayal, rage, and vengeance, all served with cold, determined detachment, all urges driven by grief and unrequited love.

That was the saddest thing about fate's entire map, really. Not Ruby's wasting in Kumara or Stone's loss of a child—those were only symptoms of a young Aiofe's own sacrifice. She hadn't wanted her crown. But once it was thrust upon her, a once-glittering path became one of shadow and death, the crown a heavy thing of stars and moonlight and obsidian stones that weighed like a universe on her brow.

And through all those shattered memories, Aiofe's undying, unrequited love for the fae princess Lyonnara bled through.

"Not just ill-fated, that love," Enyali whispered to the bundle in her arms. "But impossible. And yet she loves that fae princess still. Feeds her magic so she can cling to life in the Darkness."

She pitied Aiofe even as she admired her. Hollowing out a veiled patch of realm within the Stygian Darkness was one thing; keeping it sustained was another. Yet the queen gave her power freely to her dying friend, without thought for the sacrifice to her own magic. And that one act cracked the shell of worlds and worlds again.

Such was the tapestry of lives and loves, that a single beat of a moth's wing might shatter the glass ceiling of the universe. The shards were even now falling and embedding in the soil of both the Stygian Darkness and the Iron Kingdom.

But none of Aiofe's grief or Ruby's sacrifice needed to touch this child of the earthen realm. Enyali had done what she could to keep the infant's world shielded. She had told Aiofe how to exact her vengeance, knowledge Aiofe traded for one mercy: granting Ruby a moment of true happiness with her mate.

Those things had sent cracks along the seams of the worlds, but they had not shattered the globe. They were nothing compared to the generations Ruby would waste before she gained enough power to see Stone again.

Enyali high-stepped over a fallen log as she considered how her gift to her sister had widened the path of Aiofe's journey toward the Shadow Court, but she did not feel guilt. The things she had set in motion were worth her sister finding love—choosing love instead of hate. Finding light in the darkness. And in doing so, Ruby had given her daughter a future.

Enyali saw Ilianna's path too. Here in the mortal realm, she saw wars and raids and human men preying on the women of her kind until the babe herself forged her own version of the Nocturnes in the human realm. Not a court of fae shadows, but a mortal echo of them, but women who would shape their own fate with grit instead of magic. The spark of her sidhe heritage would live in her blood, guided by Enyali's hand. Hard as they were to foresee, some destinies refused to be altered. Sometimes all paths led to the same destination.

But at least these pathways were separate now. Fae and Human. Magic and mortal. Unlinked. Liberated from each other. That was how Ruby wanted it. She understood Stone's human magic. She knew the babe's greatest strength would be forged in hardship, shaped in her fight to survive. The way the sisters used their own muscle and sinew against each other instead of spells. There was power in that. Mortals understood how to thrive despite themselves. And this babe would thrive.

The visions had been strong even in Kumara, and they had forced the seeress to act. For Ruby. For Stone. For the infant. And she had acted, no matter the cost. She could not know truly that one destiny was meant to brush against another before parting again. She knew only enough to guide her into the woods with this child in her arms.

"Aiofe couldn't know, you see," she said, peering down into the pink face that stared up at her, briefly soothed by her voice. "But she knows now. And she will have her vengeance. She is patient."

A smile lifted the babe's lips, drawing a sigh from the seer. "And I am patient as well. As your mother is. She will thrall for the queen for a time, but she will find her body again, see your father again. Of that, have no doubt, my small thing."

Unspooling like frayed thread, the visions ran faster than she could shape into language. They bade her to play an unwitting part, and she believed fate had manipulated her too—tangling past, present, and future into a garbled knot.

Images of a king and his greed for power. Flashes of a mortal woman with black hair and wild eyes and a desire for revenge so sharp it cut her throat from the inside. And behind her mind's eye, Ruby clawing her way toward the upper realms because that black-haired mortal raged her way through Fae.

But the visions were tangled too tightly to tease into straight timelines. She only knew they were connected somehow, and that the fae realms were no longer hers to worry over.

Because this infant—this human thing that softened her insides like bone-marrow jelly and filled her with a terror of losing her—this was her duty now.

Enyali stepped over a fallen log covered in fungus and moss and clutched her sister's child closer.

"So many lives lost," she rasped. "So many more to lose." She inhaled the sweet daylight air, so different from the scent of blood and moon and the stale breath of the Darkness. The vastness of it overwhelmed her, more than she ever imagined after so long in the Nocturnes and that hateful temple of shadow.

She looked down at the mortal she had helped bring into the worlds, a smile moving across her face.

All that work to bring her to the lands of mortals, but she was worth it. One fine thing born of anger and vengeance. A thing of innocence and hope.

She was beautiful. And strong. And fierce. She had fought Enyali many times on their journey from the world of shadows, through woods and bracken.

Twice, Enyali had to stop to truss the small creature up in fabrics tight enough to keep her arms and legs from flailing out of her unpracticed grip. But the constant battle was a balm to the seer's spirit. So much like Ruby, this small thing. Mortal and vulnerable as she was, she had a sidhe heart full of spit and rage.

And that spirit would birth strength in this primitive human world. While ungainly mortals built their homes of stone and thatch and huddled behind wooden fences and trenches, Enyali would teach her the ways of the Nocturnes. One small creature with a destiny that stretched into realms even Enyali's vision could not reach.

But she knew one thing. No matter what the future held, Ruby's child—Stone's child—would thrive.

Enyali would make sure of it.

***

Thanks so much for spending time with *A Serpent in the Embers*. I hope you loved the tragic tale of romance. If this is your first peek into the world of the Iron Kingdom, and are dying to know about the 'mortal woman with black hair and wild eyes who possesses a desire for revenge so sharp it was like glass in her throat', you'll find an entire, bingeable series waiting to unfold for you. Filled with enemies to lovers vibes and a slow, aching burn, you might be excited to revisit some familiar characters in her journey. Start with Realm of Ash.

I WANT TO THANK all my regular ARC readers, who are too numerous to post, but some true regulars like Evelyn Dotson, Caroline Jenkins, and Denise Sherman come to mind. Some newish readers joined us and deserve thanks as well. Ana Spanovic, Jessica Aranda, Betsy Brooks, and Val Ackroyd.

Special thanks to Debra Martin (who writes romance under the name Debra L. Martin) and Julie Pederick who helped find those pesky spots where continuity floundered and where the romance slackened. You made such a difference in the story and I can't thank you enough.

I appreciate you so much

-t-

www.ingramcontent.com/pod-product-compliance
Lightning Source LLC
Chambersburg PA
CBHW030630120726
47904CB00006B/2106